# HAUNTED HISTORY

## RICH RAINEY

WARNER BOOKS

A Time Warner Company

## Acknowledgments

I'd like to thank Nicholas Westbrook for sharing his expertise on the history of Fort Ticonderoga and the legend of Duncan Campbell; John Dutcher and Phil Chase for their insights on Forge; and John McCarty for first telling me the tale of Haitian revolutionary Charlemagne Peralte.

Special thanks to Brian Thomsen at Warner Books for his encouragement throughout this project.

WARNER BOOKS EDITION

Cover photograph by Jeff Potter
Cover design by Diane Luger

Warner Books, Inc.
1271 Avenue of the Americas
New York, NY 10020

W A Time Warner Company

Printed in the United States of America

First Printing: October, 1992

10  9  8  7  6  5  4  3  2  1

# HISTORICAL SHOCKERS THEY DIDN'T TEACH YOU IN SCHOOL

- The haunting of the commander of the famous Black Watch Regiment from a remote castle in Scotland to a bloody American battlefield in the French and Indian War
- The awesome legends of the magicians and martial artists in the ancient Knights Templar—and the truth behind the tales
- The discovery of King Arthur's alleged resting place guide by the ghost of a medieval monk
- The conjurations and prayers of French crusader Emperor Charlemagne against the powerful infidel hordes of the Saracens
- The killing of a Haitian voodoo revolutionary by a U.S. Marine sharpshooter—with a silver bullet
- The novel that became the psychic blueprint for the notorious kidnapping of heiress Patty Hearst.

➤

## THE STORIES THAT MADE HISTORY, BUT NOT THE HISTORY BOOKS— TOLD HERE TOGETHER FOR THE FIRST TIME...

# HAUNTED HISTORY

# TABLE OF CONTENTS

# 1

# Excavations and Revelations: The Glastonbury Ghosts

## The Isles of the King

"Arthur himself, our reknowned King, was mortally wounded and was carried off to the Isle of Avalon . . ."

So writes Geoffrey of Monmouth in *History of the Kings of Britain*, which appeared in the early twelfth century. According to Geoffrey's version the year was A.D. 542, when Arthur and Modred clashed at Camlann. Many scholars have placed Arthur around A.D. 470, and some have even traced him to a pagan archetype from the misty days of prehistory.

While writers before and after Geoffrey have debated the time and place that Arthur lived—and even whether he existed or not—an equally lasting mystery is where he died and was buried. Or, for that matter, if he ever died. . . .

One of the most frequently cited resting places for Arthur is Glastonbury Abbey in Somerset, England. The

1

ruins of the abbey are situated on a high hill overlooking a small town in a valley that once was covered with water. The argument goes that since this would have made Glastonbury an island at the time of Arthur's reign, it is a plausible candidate for Avalon.

But aside from the geographical similarity between descriptions of Avalon and Glastonbury, there are other traditions that link Arthur with the site. And there is some physical evidence as well—although the meaning of the "evidence" has been a bone of contention for almost a thousand years.

## The Unearthed King

From the beginning, histories and romances alike have associated the figure of Arthur with the Holy Grail, a relic allegedly kept at Glastonbury Abbey, one of the oldest Christian sites in England. If, as many researchers have ventured, Arthur fell into the mold of a Roman-Briton war leader, *dux bellorum*, then someone in his exalted position probably would be taken to a site such as Glastonbury, where other venerated Britons were laid to rest over the centuries.

Some accounts say that Glastonbury was founded by Joseph of Arimathea, who used the Holy Grail to save the blood of Christ after his crucifixion. Then Joseph supposedly sailed to Britain with a small group of followers who guarded the Grail from then on at Glastonbury. But many researchers have denied that the Grail or Joseph ever came to Glastonbury.

And though a few locations in France as well as several other sites in Britain, including the Isle of Man, have been "identified" as Avalon, the hallowed ground of Glastonbury has something much more concrete to offer as evidence.

In the year 1184, Glastonbury was destroyed by fire, following which the monks started a lengthy rebuilding process. Seven years later, in 1191, the Abbot of Glastonbury directed a number of monks to dig at a certain spot in one of the old cemeteries. After uncovering several layers of earth, they struck a large stone cross upon which archaic Latin characters were etched. The translation reads: "Here lies buried the reknowned King Arthur in the island of Avalon." The monks continued digging several feet deeper, until they finally struck a huge coffin that was centuries old.

Made of a hollow tree trunk, the coffin contained the skeleton of an exceedingly large man. A deep wound in the skull and another in the leg had apparently caused the man's death.

But he was not alone.

Also in the coffin were strands of blond hair and the much smaller bones of a woman.

Arthur and Guinevere had been found at last, exactly where the myths and legend placed them. At least, that was the story the monks told, and from that point on visitors to Glastonbury Abbey recorded the find.

Nearly a century later, the bones were dug up once again on the orders of King Edward I, who wished to verify for himself that such renowned relics existed at the site. There the prized relics remained for the next few hundred years, until the entire site was looted during the religious purge of the Reformation.

The bones were gone—but the spirit of Arthur still lived on in the legends that promised the Return of the King who was said just to be sleeping in the subterranean depths of Avalon.

But other spirits were also working their magic on the holy spot. And detailed records of these spirits were kept, thanks to Frederick Bligh Bond, who began another series of excavations at Glastonbury in 1907 when he was hired by the Church of England, which now owned the historic site.

## Bligh Bond and Avalon

An architect and archaeologist, Bligh Bond was interested in Avalon even before he went to work for the Church of England. The place had a mystical appeal to him, an attraction that would last long after he was dismissed for performing his duty a bit too well.

Not only did Bond uncover hidden chapels and catacombs that proved that the site was much larger than anyone had previously guessed, but he brought to light the activities of a number of monks—dead for hundreds of years—who guided him in the incredible project.

Though he kept this spiritual guidance a secret, Bond immediately had great success.

Basing his initial work on what he told his superiors and the public was nothing more than instinct, Bond began excavating an area far to the east of the abbey where he uncovered the foundations of a chapel. For the next fifteen years, he and his crew continued to have success in unearthing ancient courtyards and catacombs on the ground of Glastonbury Abbey.

Since it was such a rich archaeological and religious site, Bond could have spent a lifetime digging at the site. But he made the mistake of telling the truth to the world about his unorthodox excavations.

All through the project, Bligh Bond claimed he had been guided by the spirits of long-dead monks of Glastonbury. Two of the more prominent ones, William and Johanne, had given him and his associates spectral specifications. Using mediumship and automatic writing, the ghostly monks dictated the outline of the world under the abbey.

Bond was quite precise in his claims and descriptions of the monks. In *The Gate of Remembrance* and *The Company of Avalon*, he explained how this mystical connection had guided him every step of the way.

Both of Bond's books attracted a huge readership, as well as censorship. The Church considered his views to be blasphemous and refused to credit any of his discoveries. A few years after his first book came out, Bond was removed from the project.

Although Bond might well have predicted the outcome of the publication of his books, it seems he was more interested in getting the truth out to the public—or the truth as he perceived it.

Ironically, Glastonbury had been held in such high regard because it had a tradition of being a place where mystical events could happen. One reason Arthur was sent to Glastonbury—or the Isle of Avalon—after the battle at Camlann was the hope that he could be miraculously healed there. After all, it was the site where the Grail was said to be. The site from which Christianity first flowed across Britain. In such a spiritually charged place, why couldn't Bond receive spiritual revelations?

But the world was not willing to hear him out. There were charges that Bond had imagined the ghostly guides or even fabricated them in the hopes of advancing the spiritualist cause. But in light of his respectable position before the books came out, the success of his excavations, and the testimony of his associates who'd also received communications from the monks, it seems fair to say that Bond was simply moved by the spirit of Glastonbury.

# 2

# A Tale of
# Two Charlemagnes

## I The King of the Franks

### Charlemagne and the City of God

In a time when kings were often pale shadows of the warlords of old, Charlemagne restored a regal presence to the throne when he inherited the kingdom of Gaul in the year 768 from his father, Pepin the Short.

Charlemagne *looked* the part of a great king who could inspire or frighten the lesser kings of Europe to follow his lead. His friend and biographer, Einhard the Frank, described Charlemagne as a tall, fair-haired man with a thick neck and a good nature, a man with a thirst for knowledge and a talent for war. As soon as he became king, Charlemagne initiated a number of campaigns that would eventually expand his borders to include much of present-day France, Germany, Holland, Belgium, and Italy.

Often viewing his wars as a struggle between Christian forces and devil-worshiping heathens and barbarians, Charlemagne was extremely convincing about spreading the word of God to all who fell under his borders. Consequently, life under his rule was literally a two-edged sword.

Conquered subjects were given a choice of converting to Christianity and, like Charlemagne, professing faith to the Prince of Peace—or having their heads cut off. Such evangelical furor caused repeated problems within Charlemagne's empire, particularly among the Saxons, who quite rationally agreed to become converts—until Charlemagne's forces left Saxon land, whereupon they would take up their ways and their wars, raiding throughout the land that Charlemagne had taken from them.

Charlemagne also fought Arabs, Basques, Lombards, and Danes with awesome regularity, though he was quite flexible about the need for Christianity where his empire bordered Spain. In his great campaign into Spain, which formed the basis for the Song of Roland, Charlemagne was actually moving south to form an alliance with one Arab army to join them in their fight against an Arabic empire that was moving north.

Though he was reportedly a pious man and was responsible for building cathedrals and monasteries all across his empire and providing for their support and protection, Charlemagne was often cavalier about matters of Christian morals when it came to his own conduct. Because of his many wives, mistresses, and children, Charlemagne may very well be considered the father of much of modern France and Germany. Aside from this often erratic Christianity, Charlemagne had a sincere interest in establishing a system of justice across the land, and made it possible for average citizens to air their grievances at his court.

This civilizing influence was made possible only by the incredible size of the armies he could muster from all corners of his empire. But in order to keep his frontier vassals loyal, Charlemagne frequently had to launch expeditions on all of his frontiers. Throughout his long reign there was seldom a moment of peace in the empire—whether because of a rebellion on the borderlands or a new war of expansion.

Though Charlemagne established a number of bishoprics throughout the empire, and often followed the counsel of Alcuin and other monks at his court, he considered himself the ultimate voice in matters of rule—whether secular or religious. This philosophy was illustrated by the way he combined the center of his earthly and heavenly empire under one roof.

While Charlemagne had many regal estates, he most often held court at Aachen (Aix-la-Chapelle), a town situated on what is now modern Germany's western border. Here Charlemagne had a chapel constructed that still stands today as part of the great cathedral of the same name.

At Aachen, Charlemagne assembled the best and brightest of the empire, bringing monks and scholars such as Alcuin and Einhard side by side with the soldiers and warlords who carried out his expeditions. He was convinced that knowledge was as important as martial skills in maintaining the empire and giving his people a balanced outlook on the world they were ruling in God's name. More interested in performance than position, he promoted reading and instruction in the sciences for nobles and commoners alike.

Einhard, in his *Life of Charlemagne*, mentions Charlemagne's special interest in astrology. Some writers use this to cast Charlemagne in an occult light, claiming that he used the stars to map out the heavens as well as his military campaigns.

Throughout his reign, Charlemagne often found himself the court of last resort for the papacy, which was always in trouble and featured a cast of popes often besieged by their own subjects. Though Charlemagne frequently came to the rescue of Pope Leo III, who was the constant victim of murder plots by rivals and his own subjects, the emperor usually took a matter-of-fact approach with the popes, often instructing *them* how to carry out their offices.

Charlemagne considered himself the true voice of the empire, with the word of the pope a formality. His interpretation of civil and secular matters was what really mattered. Since this was a time when candidates for the papal throne often resorted to murder and conspiracy to win office, he saw no need to have the crown bestowed on him by the pope. But he allowed it to happen, and so endowed his empire with the official backing of the Christian church.

Just as Saint Augustine's book *The City of God* advanced the idea that Rome was the earthly residence for

God's own messengers, Charlemagne believed that his empire was like the City of God, and he the divinely ordained ruler. Charlemagne was not only the worldly king, but he was the ultimate representative of God on earth, though he accepted this as merely one more symbol of the Holy Roman Empire he was rebuilding.

As mentioned above, this godliness took a bizarre turn when Charlemagne went about converting the Saxons.

## The Sacred Saxon Tree

Throughout Charlemagne's forty-six-year reign, the most stubborn resistance came from Saxon warriors on his northern border who fought against his constant expansion into their homeland. Once conquered, they rarely stayed conquered for long. As soon as Charlemagne's armies withdrew from the area, or if other Saxons rode to their side with reinforcements, the Saxons usually renounced whatever alliance the emperor had pressed them into.

Like the Vikings who would prowl on the borders of Charlemagne's empire toward the end of his reign, the Saxons often attacked churches and monasteries, ransacking them of their treasures and killing the inhabitants. The Christians saw these as devil-inspired acts, blasphemy of the worst sort.

But to the Saxons, the churches were the symbols of the destruction of their way of life and the rich treasures they held nothing more than plunder from the sacking of *their* lands. It was hard for them to take seriously a religion that offered peace and salvation on one hand, and a severed head on the other.

In *The Life of Charlemagne*, written fifteen years after the emperor's death, Einhard discussed this brutal war that lasted for thirty-three years. According to Einhard, the war could have ended much sooner if the Saxons had just negotiated in good faith. "Sometimes they . . . promised to abandon their devil worship and submit willingly to the Christian faith . . . Hardly a year passed in which they did not vacillate between surrender and defiance."

In later years, one of Charlemagne's solutions to this problem was to forcibly relocate thousands of Saxons to far corners of the empire.

Another "solution" was to have them killed en masse. In the year 782, in an act that horrified many of his own advisers, Charlemagne had nearly five thousand Saxons decapitated at Verdun, baptising the nearby river with blood. This horrendous massacre also shocked the enraged warriors of Saxony, who continued their war for twenty more years.

But one of the most brutal acts in the eyes of the Saxons was Charlemagne's desecration of *their* religious altar— known as the Irminsul. This great tree in the middle of a sacred grove was the center of worship for the Saxons. Here in the woods their gods were celebrated. Armor and offerings hung from the sacred boughs of Irminsul, harking back to pagan traditions when such trees symbolized the heart and soul of a warrior race and were often festooned with the skulls of their enemies and the plunder they had taken.

According to Saxon belief, the Irminsul was the tree that held the sky above.

Charlemagne struck deep at the heart of the Saxons, destroying their grove but not their worship.

As evidenced by the martial fervor of the Christian warriors, this tree represented nothing more than the superstitions of a barbaric lot—even though the Christian soldiers had superstitions of their own.

## The Mystic and Martial Arts

One of the prized relics said to be in Charlemagne's possession was the Spear of Longinus. Several contemporary historians have traced the spear that pierced the side of Christ on the cross to Visigoth and Frankish kings, and subsequently to the regalia that Charlemagne inherited.

Since the days of Constantine, this spear supposedly accompanied Holy Roman Emperors into battle, helping their hosts to victory. According to a history written by William of Malmesbury, whenever Charlemagne hurled the spear in the direction of his enemies it would cause them to fall back, and bring about an inevitable victory for the Christian armies.

Whether it was through the force endowed in the spear, or the force of his own willpower, Charlemagne was the first ruler in his line to expand the boundaries of his kingdom into what could be considered an empire. Later, upon being crowned emperor by Pope Leo III, he completed the circle by inaugurating a Holy Roman Empire once more.

Trevor Ravenscroft's book *The Spear of Destiny* cites the Spear of Longinus as the source of Charlemagne's alleged clairvoyant abilities—which supposedly allowed him to see into the future.

A later German emperor, Frederick Barbarossa, also was believed to possess the Spear of Longinus. Interestingly enough, there are other parallels between Charlemagne and Frederick.

As with Arthur before him and Frederick who came after him, Charlemagne's existence so dramatically shaped the events of the world that many people found it impossible to believe that he ever died. Like these other great war kings, Charlemagne is believed merely sleeping inside a mountain somewhere, entombed until the hour of the country's greatest need, when he will return and lead his people to salvation.

This motif of great kings surviving in secret despite historical accounts of their deaths has persisted from the Camelot of King Arthur to the Camelot of JFK. But in a way, a resurrection of Charlemagne really did occur in the early twentieth century in the form of a Haitian revolutionary, Charlemagne Peralte, whose exploits are covered in the second part of this chapter.

Whether or not Charlemagne possessed the actual Spear of Longinus, the fact remains that his biographer, Einhard, attached great significance to the spear that the emperor carried. Einhard discusses the role the spear played in one instance as an omen of the emperor's death. Appropriately enough, the Saxons figure in this incident.

Charlemagne had begun his wars against the Saxons with a bit of religious warfare—the cutting down of Irminsul. Now once again he was marching off to fight against the Saxons when an omen of his death was written in the sky.

As Einhard wrote in *The Life of Charlemagne*: "Just before sunrise, as he was setting out from his camp and was beginning the day's march, he suddenly saw a meteor flash down from the heavens and pass across the clear sky from right to left with a great blaze of light."

Through his wars of expansion, Charlemagne looked heavenward for support and sustenance. Toward the end of his reign there were a number of omens hinting at his impending death—but they were omens he chose to ignore.

As the riders around him stared up at the sky, Charlemagne's horse suddenly dropped out from under him, scattering his weapons and armor on the ground. The spear was literally knocked from his grasp by a bolt that scarred the heavens.

Einhard attaches great significance to the fact that the spear that Charlemagne carried with him on his expeditions was cast more than twenty feet away from him by the fall. To the mystically inclined, nothing could be more symbolic of the emperor's so dramatically losing his connection to the divine throne.

Other omens Einhard writes about include a number of earthquakes that suddenly occurred in Aachen, Charlemagne's own City of God where he'd built his great cathedral. The cathedral itself bore witness to a more specific omen. According to Einhard, the inscription in the cathedral that named Charlemagne as the man who built it, faded and became illegible a few months before he died.

Along with Einhard's down-to-earth recollections of Charlemagne, there are recorded several intriguing events surrounding the emperor. Notker the Stammer's biography of Charlemagne includes some quite factual data about the emperor's reign, but at the same time the monk's own religious twist on matters shows up in many passages that are startling to a modern-day reader.

Notker often wrote quite fabulous statements in a stunningly calm manner. For example, in one passage he writes, "A certain devil of the type called hobgoblins . . . had the habit of visiting the dwelling of a local blacksmith." Likewise, a number of bishops and clergymen are regularly victimized by shaggy devils and witches that occur frequently in Notker's account. Notker even writes about a group of giants descended from the same race of giants mentioned in the Bible, who are plotting against Charlemagne's scions.

These amazing reports are often followed by quite specific records of military campaigns that include place names and names of knights awarded honor for service in Charlemagne's army.

While much of Notker's account reads like spurious parables, he captures the military presence of Charlemagne's warriors in passages that are far removed from the chivalrous tint of so many other "historical" writings.

Writing about one of Charlemagne's more prominent warriors, a man named Eishere who sounds like a real-life counterpart to Robert E. Howard's Conan the Barbarian, Notker describes Eishere as a tall man on a great horse who waded into the ranks of Avars and Bohemians and "spitted them on his spear as if they were tiny birds."

Notker also captures the image of Charlemagne, who often led his troops into battle with his spear: "Then came in sight that man of iron, Charlemagne, topped with his iron helm, his fists in iron gloves . . . An iron spear raised high against the sky he gripped in his left hand, while in his right, he held his still unconquered sword."

Because of his possession of the sacred relic believed to be the Spear of Longinus, and other prized artifacts, including a grail and some of Christ's blood, a number of writers have also linked Charlemagne to the royal bloodline of the Grail family, which supposedly claims an unbroken lineage from the House of David.

Also of great importance to Charlemagne was his sword.

Arthur had Excalibur.

Atilla had his Sword of Death.

And Charlemagne had Joyeuse, an exquisitely wrought sword that truly befitted an emperor—complete with a scabbard and hilt made of solid gold.

Many other writers besides Einhard and Notker wrote about Charlemagne, but their "histories" are often more fancy than fact. For example, in Archbishop Turpin's account of one of Charlemagne's campaigns—where the Christian armies are blessed with the opportunity to slaughter thousands of infidels—he writes of Charlemagne's soldiers planting their spears upright in the ground, only to have them instantly take root and spring up into a forest of living trees.

Some of the stories are outright fables. Others are examples of finely tooled propaganda, such as the heavenly letter to Charlemagne's father, Pepin the Short, that was supposedly dictated to the pope by Saint Peter. Since Pepin the Short revered Saint Peter, this letter was calculated to get him to bring his troops to Rome with greater speed.

As mentioned in Lynn Thorndike's *History of Medieval Europe*, the letter sent to Pepin was both mystical and mercenary at once. If Pepin sent his armies to conquer the Lombards besieging the pope, then Pepin and his people would prosper and get into heaven. But if they didn't listen to the plea, the gates of heaven would be closed to them.

Thorndike links this letter to the forgery known as the Donation of Constantine, which the church used to claim lands spread across Europe that were supposedly ceded by Constantine to Pope Sylvester after the pope miraculously cured him of leprosy.

## The Song of Roland

Charlemagne ultimately succeeded in crushing rebellions inside his borders, but by no means was he invincible. The Saxons had their victories over him, as well as the Danes, whose plundering raids often went unchecked. But one of the most crushing defeats in Charlemagne's history has passed on into legend as the basis of the epic *Song of Roland*.

After an expedition into Spain to fight the Saracens—a name applied to just about any enemy of the Christianized empire—Charlemagne was forced to pull back across the Pyrenees into France to deal with uprisings on his northern borders.

Charlemagne left Roland, Warden of the Breton Marches, in charge of the rear guard. As the rear guard moved into the pass at Roncesvalles, an army of Basques who were allied with Charlemagne suddenly fell upon the rear guard from all sides. They annihilated Roland's force and plundered the baggage train.

The image of Roland blowing the horn, calling the rest of Charlemagne's army back to Roncesvalles, has passed on into legend. And so has the alleged dream that Charlemagne had before the battle. In this dream Charlemagne saw a great catastrophe befalling his army and offered to provide Roland with considerable reinforcements.

But the proud Roland refused, a medieval Custer so certain of his martial ability that to accept help would be an insult. As a result, the rear guard was destroyed. And Charlemagne's dream of disaster came to pass.

*The Song of Roland* also introduced other miraculous deeds surrounding Charlemagne, including angelic hordes riding with them in battle and God holding back the night long enough for Charlemagne's army to destroy the treacherous horde that ambushed Roland.

\* \* \*

Another mystical relic allegedly in the hands of Charlemagne was a book known as The Enchiridion, a collection of prayers and charms to summon angelic spirits and ward off evils.

As explained in Lewis Spence's classic *Encyclopedia of the Occult*, the book was supposedly given to Charlemagne by Pope Leo, who owed so much to the man he had crowned emperor. As a result of devoutly employing the prayers of the book, it was believed, Charlemagne always had good fortune. Since Charlemagne was known to place great stock in the benefits of reading divinely inspired texts, such a book—if it existed—would certainly find a good home at Aachen.

In light of Charlemagne's good fortune—and his unique approach to the codes of Christianity—perhaps this volume of enchantments really was one more weapon in the emperor's arsenal.

## II *The Return of Charlemagne*

### The Haitian Patriot

Eleven hundred years after Charlemagne's death, another Charlemagne appeared on the world stage. He, too, was a nationalist leader. But rather than inherit the reins of empire, guerrilla leader Charlemagne Peralte fought against foreign empires who were deciding the fate of Haiti.

Although Peralte assumed a leadership role in the revolutionary army in 1918, the conditions that brought him to the fore began a few years earlier.

In the year 1915, far removed from the battlefields in Europe where World War I was raging, the Caribbean island of Haiti had once again become of great interest to the great powers involved in that overseas war.

Germany, France, and the United States recognized the strategic importance of Haiti, particularly its harbor of Môle St.-Nicholas. With Haiti heavily indebted to all three countries and its economy in a state of chaos, there was a chance of military intervention from any or all of them.

To the United States, the port represented a severe threat to its southeast border if it fell under German control. The widespread unrest in Haiti was also considered a threat to American citizens and their holdings. Yet another influence was the Monroe Doctrine, which in the early decades of the twentieth century was interpreted as a license for U.S. intervention in any country in the Americas.

But even as the international powers began their maneuvers to draw Haiti into the orbit of their struggle, an equally powerful force was also at work throughout Haiti—the need to be free. This tradition of freedom was bound to collide with the interests of whatever world power tried to gain control over Haiti.

For more than one hundred years after the Haitians defeated Napoleon's army of thirty thousand soldiers sent to subdue the slave rebellion, the island had been governing itself.

## The Citadelle

In 1804, the French troops had been decimated by the Haitian forces marshaled by Jean Jacques Dessalines, Toussaint L'Ouverture, and Henri Christophe.

Soon after the remnants of the French army fled the island, Henri Christophe emerged as the leader of the northern half of the country and had himself crowned emperor. To defend himself against any renewed French invasion, Christophe began constructing the immense fortress known as the Citadelle deep within the mountains south of Cap-Haïtien.

This fortress, which still stands today, took the lives of thousands of Haitians forced to work on it under horrible conditions. And as a result it has become not only a symbol of Haitian resistance to outside forces, but also of the internal struggles that have brought tragedy to the island ever since.

While Christophe was admired as a leader in the war against the French, a man around whom legend has cast an almost supernatural aura, his regal excesses soon caused his own people to rise up against him. After suffering a stroke, Christophe took his own life by shooting himself in the heart.

According to legend, Christophe used a silver bullet when he committed suicide.

## The Seeds of Revolution

About one hundred years later Charlemagne Peralte, a former army officer, began leading his people against another invasion. Charlemagne came to the fore as a leader in 1918 when he commanded a large force of *cacos*, as the guerrilla troops based in the interior were called.

The cacos fought against the American occupation troops as well as the Haitian gendarmerie, which was directed by the marines. They also fought against the government of Haitian president Philippe Sudre Dartiguenave, which was established and controlled by U.S. occupation forces.

During Dartiguenave's administration, the Haitian government became a protectorate of the United States. It was also during his administration that a practice known as *corvee* was reinstituted, which led to widespread revolt among the peasant population. Originally this policy required peasants from each district to devote a certain number of hours toward civil projects in their area.

But as the policy was enforced by the marines and the gendarmes, it practically became a form of legalized slavery in which men were taken from their villages and forced to work under abominable conditions that often led to their deaths.

To the Haitians who were pressed into this "voluntary" work force, it seemed a hopeless situation. If they submitted to the corvee, they might be abandoning their families, never to return. If they resisted the "recruitment" efforts, they might be beaten or shot.

Consequently, many of the Haitians found another alternative—armed resistance. They moved to the deep hills of the interior—staying ahead of the roads that corvee crews were building closer and closer to the guerrilla strongholds in the mountainous interior.

Atrocities were committed on all sides—gendarmes against the Haitian citizenry, marines against cacos and civilians, and cacos against U.S. forces and gendarmes. While many Haitians considered the cacos to be lawless bandits, others looked to them for salvation from this new form of slavery.

The cacos' fierce resistance to Dartiguenave's government and the U.S. forces backing it was strengthened by the supernatural beliefs of the guerrillas. Most of the leaders of the movement and their followers practiced voodoo rites and concocted potions that were believed to make them invincible in battle.

As the leader of a large guerrilla army of cacos that survived war with the marines and gendarmes for nearly two years, Charlemagne assumed a majestic and magical character in the eyes of his followers.

While the occupation troops no doubt brought a stability to certain parts of the island republic and began a program of modernization, their presence also fostered an intense bitterness that galvanized the opposition.

The first U.S. occupation troops arrived in Haiti in July of 1915 when Admiral Caperton landed at Port-au-Prince and immediately took control of the Haitian capital.

But there were indications in the American press long

before that the marines were coming. For example, on January 17, 1915, *The New York Times* ran an article about Haitian revolutionaries led by General Vilbrun Guillaume taking peaceful control of Cap-Haïtien.

The article also reports the response from the United States, which was asked by foreign consuls in the area to send in marines to protect the interests of foreigners in Cap-Haïtien. ''The gunboat Wheeling is at Port-au-Prince. The armored cruiser Washington is now speeding . . . with a large force of marines for Guanacayabo Bay . . .''

As Guillaume moved south toward Port-au-Prince, the U.S. forces also concentrated on the area. On February 2, a force of six hundred marines on the cruiser *Montana* began patrolling the waters off Port-au-Prince. Admiral Caperton's flagship, the USS *Washington*, also moved to the capital.

By February 24, the current Haitian president, Davilmar Theodor, sought asylum on the Dutch steamer *Frederik Hendrik* in the waters of Port-au-Prince. Two days later the revolutionary leader General Guillaume assumed the role of the presidency—at the time the most dangerous position a man could hold.

The country was in a state of near anarchy owing to the war between political leaders and the army factions backing them. Within the past four years, seven presidents had ruled Haiti—all of them violently removed from office.

In the summer of 1915, history began repeating itself when revolutionary leader Rosalvo Bobo waged a campaign against the presidency of Guillaume. With headlines reminiscent of Guillaume's revolt against the presidency, the newspapers on June 28 reported that seven hundred marines were sailing to Cap-Haïtien to relieve the force of French marines that had landed there to maintain order.

The conflict exploded on July 28 just after President Guillaume had 160 of his political enemies massacred, including the ex-president of Haiti. This action caused a mass uprising against Guillaume, who fled for his life to the French embassy in Port-au-Prince.

But when the mob discovered Guillaume was there, they dragged him out of the embassy and shot him. Then they dismembered him and paraded through the streets, displaying parts of his body like trophies of war.

The USS *Washington* landed in the capital with a force of over three hundred marines. By then Bobo had assembled a revolutionary force of fifteen hundred men to bolster *his* claim to the presidency.

However, Admiral Caperton landed hundreds of additional marines on the island who immediately began disarming the revolutionaries and creating a constabulary of Haitians to help keep order. In such a climate of chaos, many of the Haitian citizens actually welcomed the arrival of the marines—although just as many were wary about their real intentions.

## Charlemagne's Reign

Charlemagne Peralte rose to prominence in 1918, largely due to his military skill and charismatic presence.

A strong, decisive leader, his cause was helped by the harsh corvee practices that sent an ever-growing number of Haitians into the ranks of the guerrillas.

Peralte's army has been estimated as being up to five thousand strong. But this nucleus of armed guerrillas was bolstered by a support group of tens of thousands more.

Like many of the voodoo-inspired cacos, Peralte cultivated an air of invulnerability about him as he led the guerrillas in attacks on marines and gendarmes, venturing down from his mountain stronghold in an area known as Hinche the Accursed to battle the occupation forces and then vanish in the wilderness.

Tales of Charlemagne Peralte's resistance and his victories spread rapidly across the island, drawing in new recruits and making him the number-one target of the marines. But the ghostlike guerrilla vanished again and again, only to show up elsewhere to strike at the enemy.

Charlemagne Peralte was unkillable—until two American officers, Captain Hannigan and Lieutenant Button, went out on their own and traveled deep into the Haitian interior. After rendezvousing with a group of gendarmes, the two officers blackened their faces and moved unnoticed into the guerrilla realm. They captured a number of cacos and found out the location of Peralte's hideout. Once again they were able to penetrate deep into the area, passing through five outposts before encountering a sentry, whom they killed.

Then they moved on to Peralte's cabin, where a bonfire was raging. According to the December 7, 1919, account of the assassination, Peralte came out from his cabin "and stood with his back toward them at the fire warming his hands. Hannigan drew his automatic revolver and fired twice, both bullets passing through the bandit chief's heart. In the excitement which followed the shooting, the two officers got safely away."

## A Legion of Legends

The original accounts of the death of Charlemagne Peralte differed in a number of respects. Some of the reports were taken from people who arrived in the United States from Haiti shortly after the killing.

Other accounts surfaced, saying that Peralte was sitting by a cooking fire with his girlfriend when the marines shot him through the heart.

Though the specifics might never be known, what *is* known is that Marine Captain Hanneken and Lieutenant Button managed to track Peralte into the heart of his wilderness stronghold and then shot him through the heart. To prove that the invincible leader was dead, they took a photograph of his corpse and hung it on a door like a crucifixion.

While contemporary reports in *The New York Times* and other papers are matter-of-fact regarding the death of Peralte, several later accounts—books and pamphlets by veterans of the military occupation—added more fantastic details to the growing legend of Charlemagne. One of the more intriguing legends surrounding the death of Peralte involves silver bullets penetrating the supernatural shield he'd thrown around himself through magical rites of voodoo.

## The War Drags On

The political struggle continued long after Charlemagne Peralte's death, although the caco forces repeatedly suffered heavy losses in their attacks on government-held towns and marine outposts.

In January of 1920, a force of three hundred cacos attacked Port-au-Prince. According to Colonel J. H. Russell, the commander of the marine and gendarme forces, more than half of the caco army was destroyed in the attack. In October of that same year, a number of other bandit chiefs—as the leaders of the cacos were called—were killed in skirmishes with marines and gendarmes.

As the occupation stretched on, more and more accounts of atrocities reached the United States, eventually arousing the public, a number of politicians, and marine commanders to call for an investigation. The impending investigations resulted in the court-martial or transfer of several marines.

An October 5, 1920, *New York Times* article discussed the atrocities. Harry A. Franck, the *Times* travel correspondent and authority on the Caribbean, attributed these acts to certain rogue elements of the marines:

"How American marines, largely made up of and officered by Southerners, opened fire with machine guns from airplanes upon defenseless Haitian villages, killing men, women, and children in the open market places; how natives were slain for 'sport' by a hoodlum element among these same Southerners, and how the ancient corvee system of enforced labor was revived and ruthlessly executed . . ."

On October 14, 1920, results of a report on the atrocities by Marine Brigadier General George Barnett were made public, addressing charges that marines engaged in "indiscriminate killing" of Haitian natives as well as large-scale execution of prisoners.

The report revealed that 3,250 Haitians were killed in the period from July 1915 to June 1920—half of them in attacks on Port-au-Prince and related operations. At the same time, two marine officers and twelve enlisted men were killed, along with twenty-six men wounded in action.

The disparity in numbers was attributed to the cacos' belief in their invulnerability—which was catastrophically proven wrong when they fell en masse beneath machine-gun fire. Many of the cacos also had old and poorly maintained weapons; a good number of them relied on scythes or machetes to go into battle.

Along with denouncing the brutal enforcement of the corvee system, Barnett also pointed out that records indicating guilt or involvement of a number of marines in such activities had mysteriously disappeared.

In *The New York Times* on October 14, 1920, Major General John A. Lejeune, Commandant of the Marine

Corps, is quoted as saying that the privates who executed captured bandits were following the orders of Lieutenant H. R. Brokaw, "who subsequently was adjudged insane and removed from the service."

At the same time, caco ambushers also committed atrocities on marines, Haitian gendarmes, and native couriers, often beheading them, cutting out their hearts, and mutilating their bodies. There were reports of a marine's heart being eaten by the cacos who'd killed him, as well as reports of cacos' stirring their rifle sights in the brains of slain marines to magically improve their shooting ability.

There are several other tales of magic and voodoo occurring in Haiti during the occupation, but one of the most intriguing accounts concerns occupation forces encountering a phantomlike entity in the woods.

In his book *The Serpent and the Rainbow*, Wade Davis writes about a tradition near the town of Saut d'Eau that involves apparitions of the Virgin Mary. One instance occurred during the American occupation. According to Davis, after being urged on by a local priest, an American captain ordered a Haitian soldier to shoot at the brilliant light surrounding the apparition. But the light danced overhead, unharmed by any of the shots, and eventually transformed into a pigeon and flew away. However, both the priest and the captain were struck dead soon after, and the soldier went mad.

Davis's book provides a fascinating journey through the physical and psychic landscape of modern Haiti, with a wealth of scientific and spiritual detail.

\* \* \*

Just as Charlemagne Peralte resurrected the name of Charlemagne the Emperor, in recent years the guerrilla leader's image has begun reappearing all across Haiti—on coins, pictures, and paintings that show that the martyred spirit of Peralte is still alive.

# 3

# Templar Treasures

## The Accursed King

Two hundred years of glory went up in flames in the year 1314 when Jacques de Molay, Grand Master of the Knights Templar, was burned at the stake by the ironically named King Philip the Fair of France.

The same king who several years before had sent a covert force of soldiers to kidnap Pope Boniface—ultimately causing his death—had finally achieved *his* holy quest. He had destroyed the order of warrior monks who had once deemed him unfit to join their ranks.

Philip's "crusade" began in the year 1307 when he had Pope Clement V summon the Grand Master of the Templars to Paris, ostensibly to discuss a new Crusade to the Holy Land. Shortly after his arrival from Cyprus, Jacques de Molay and hundreds of other Templars were arrested. The king's men struck simultaneously all across the country, seizing the Templars and herding them away to the dungeons of Paris.

It happened to be Friday the thirteenth when Philip's trap was sprung.

Aided by the induced testimony of a defector from the Templars named Esquian de Horian, Philip charged the order of monks with heresy, idolatry, witchcraft, and several other charges conjured up by his chief henchman, William de Nogaret, a "pious" plotter who happened to be excommunicated at the time. One of the key charges leveled against the Templars was that they worshiped a mysterious head or skull hidden in their chapels.

Using gruesome torture, Philip and his devout interrogators exacted confessions from just about any Templar they'd imprisoned. Since many of the Templars died under the questioning, it's little wonder that the monks who survived the brutal treatment confessed to the outlandish charges brought against them. Even the Grand Master "confessed" to the charges.

After being imprisoned for several years, Jacques de Molay was paraded before the public to make his confession again—to prove to Philip's subjects once and for all that the charges weren't fraudulent and that the king was right in persecuting the monks.

But instead of being vindicated, the king was humiliated by the Grand Master, who used the occasion to recant his confession and tell the world how Philip's thugs had forced the confessions from him and the other Templars. The Grand Master proclaimed the innocence of the Templars and the guilt of the king.

Jacques de Molay was burned, and Philip the Fair proceeded to loot the holdings of the Templars.

But the French king received something else from the Templar Grand Master, because as he succumbed to the consuming flames at the stake, the Grand Master of the Templars cursed King Philip and Pope Clement for conspiring against the order—telling them he would see them both before God before the year was out, and that God would be their judge.

The first part of the curse came true when Pope Clement died one month later.

King Philip died within nine months of sending the Grand Master to his death, thus fulfilling the second part of the Templar's curse. But he had had plenty of time to plunder the estates of the Templars, "legitimizing" this thievery by conjuring up debts the order supposedly owed the bankrupt king. The Knights Templars' holdings had been distributed among the Church, the royal treasury, and some of the other religious orders of the day.

The persecution of the Templar order was enforced in name only across the rest of the continent, because the rulers of these countries investigated the charges of Pope Clement and King Philip and found them to be fraudulent. However, since a papal edict officially abolished the charter of the Templars and outlawed the order, the other European rulers felt obliged to pay lip service. While the order of Templars was abolished in these countries, the Templars themselves moved freely about through other orders. The Knights Hospitaler welcomed many of the

Templars into their ranks, and a good number of them appeared in Portugal as the Knights of Christ.

This disintegration—or distribution—of the warrior monks led to many rumors of a secret Knights Templar order lasting through the ages, supposedly maintaining a covert order within the groups that welcomed them into their ranks. As a result, much like the alleged secret order of the Illuminati, which is used as a scapegoat for any conspiracy theory in need of a villain, the Templars are often written about as hidden powers behind grand schemes.

Since the Templars of medieval times were in fact the first international bankers—a pet phrase among conspiracy buffs—it's easy to see how someone searching for secret manipulators could latch on to the extinct order. But the Templars became bankers simply because of the growth and capacity of their order over a two-hundred-year period. With fortresses, fleets, and temples spread across the Middle East and Europe, they were in a logical position to safeguard money as well as transfer it.

In fact, King Philip himself had turned to the Templars to safeguard the dwindling royal treasury, because they alone had the reputation of being trusted with its safekeeping.

Philip had once turned to the Templars for another reason as well. While running for his life from his own faithful subjects, Philip had had to flee to a Temple to avoid being killed. Perhaps this was one more reason why he resented them.

In many ways the Templars were more powerful than

any king in Europe. They had the ability to raise and fund Crusader armies, they had shock-troop soldiers from the order to lead them, and they had the ear of every ruler in Europe. And their temples were also safe houses.

Perhaps King Philip saw his own throne in danger from such an organization—an organization that considered themselves too virtuous to include him in their ranks. Regardless of the king's reason, he was able to carry out a successful persecution of the Templars because of their long history of secrecy. Rumor and legend had surrounded the mysterious organization ever since it was founded, ultimately providing enough rope for the king to hang them.

## Shrouded in Mystery

The Knights of the Temple of Solomon of Jerusalem, or Knights Templar as they were later known, first surfaced in the year 1118. Led by Hugh de Payens, a nobleman from Burgundy, a small cadre of nine knights was given prestigious quarters by the current ruler of Jerusalem—King Baldwin, a Crusader who assumed kingship in 1100.

Much like the legendary Solomon whose palace they were headquartered in, the Templars would become known far and wide for their sage counsel and for their courage. Taking vows of chastity and poverty—while at the same time taking up arms to fight in the name of Christianity—the Templars were initially charged with escorting pilgrims to Jerusalem. This role evolved as the ranks and reputation of the Templars grew, until eventually they became a large-scale military force that supported the Crusader armies from Europe.

Throughout two hundred years of Crusades, nobles from Europe swelled the ranks of the Templars, deeding large property and fortunes to them. Despite their individual vows of poverty, the organization became wealthy. Since the Templars had astute administrators to handle their fortunes, kings and nobles outside the order turned to them to handle their fortunes or to borrow from them, adding even more revenues to the order.

Consequently, the small band of knights grew into a multinational organization. Its reputation on the battlefield also won it international prestige. But despite the glories won beneath their banner, the Templars were swept by the tides of history. In 1291, Muslim armies destroyed the last Crusader and Templar forces at Acre, driving them from the Holy Land. The European invasions were ended, and so was the *raison d'être* of the Knights Templar.

From their base on Cyprus, the Templars now concentrated on building up their fleets and maintaining their estates all across Europe. While the Templars were still prepared to support another Crusade, chances were slim that European regents would raise armies large enough to launch another campaign.

And in the end, it wasn't an enemy army that took down the Templars. It was a French king who stabbed them in the back.

Some writers have connected the head that the Templars allegedly worshiped to the Shroud of Turin, the supposed burial cloth of Christ that somehow captured a three-dimensional image of him. When folded several times and exhibited like a portrait, this shroud supposedly bears a likeness to a bearded face that, by some accounts, appeared in the Templars' chapels. The shroud has also been linked by Ian Wilson and other writers to the Mandylion, an earlier relic of Christianity that was either the shroud that captured the image of Christ's body or a linen cloth used to wipe his face before his crucifixion.

According to the theory connecting the Shroud of Turin to the Templars, it first came into their hands during the Crusades and from then on was harbored as a sacred relic in one of their treasure houses. Since initiation into their order was private and surrounded by mystery, as were many of their services, it's possible to see how distortions of Templar practices suggesting a head or idol could spread following exhibition of the shroud. Even if the Templars did possess a shroud, was it a genuine relic or a forgery?

An October 24, 1988, article in *Time* magazine reported on tests sanctioned by Cardinal Ballestrero that dated the Shroud of Turin to a period from 1260 to 1380. The tests were independently conducted by Oxford University, the University of Arizona, and the Federal University of Technology in Zurich. Using carbon-14 dating techniques, the separate tests indicated that the shroud first appeared in the thirteenth or fourteenth century with "near absolute certainty that it dates from no earlier than 1200." According to the article, this unprecedented test was agreed to by Cardinal Ballestrero because technology had advanced to the point where relatively small samples of the shroud could be used, thus keeping the shroud intact.

This dating coincides with the time when the shroud was first exhibited by a French nobleman, Geoffrey de Charnay.

## Heads of State

While most of the charges against the Templars seem absurd at first glance, it is possible to see how some of them came about. One of the charters of the Templars was to reform knights and miscreants who had been declared persona non grata by their own people. Bernard of Clairvaux, an early patron of the Templars, wrote that at the time the order was formed many knights were regarded as little more than titled thieves who could kill, rob, and rape at their leisure. Cloaked in illusory chivalry and sponsored by nobles able to buy their way out of prosecution, knighthood had fallen low in the public's esteem. Paralleling this was the often low regard the average man felt for corrupt clergymen who engaged in the selling of indulgences, which would forgive any sin if the price was right.

It was hoped that the Knights Templar would restore the reputation of both clergy and knighthood. They were seen as a force of spiritual shock troops—monks as well as martial artists—who could transform some of the baser knights into men of virtue.

While most of the "reformed" initiates became honorable men under the discipline of the Templars, some of them stayed true to their roots and continued their criminal pursuits while cloaked in the mantle and cross of the order. Inevitably, there were a few renegade Templars included in the ranks as they grew into a worldwide military and religious order over the decades.

But to argue that the entire order was corrupt is wrong. Unfortunately, the man behind the argument, King Philip IV, had the power to make it stick. Philip and his coconspirators were devout adherents of the creed that if the lie was big enough, the public would believe it.

The Templars were accused of desecrating the cross, denying belief in Christ, practicing demon worship, practicing homosexuality, ritually murdering newborns, summoning a demonic familiar in the form of a black cat, and perhaps strangest of all—worshiping a mysterious head or skull called Baphomet.

Descriptions of the head, obtained under torture or from hearsay, varied greatly. By some accounts it was a jewel-studded skull or a talking three-faced head. According to Lewis Spence's monumental *Encyclopedia of the Occult*, "Some said it was a frightful head, with long beard and sparkling eyes; others said it was a man's skull . . . one witness described it as a painting representing the image of a man."

S. Baring-Gould, in *The Holy Grail*, writes of the idol's being described as "an old skin embalmed and polished, in which the Templar places his very vile faith and trust . . . and it has in the sockets eyes of carbuncle shining with the brightness of the sky." Baring-Gould also mentions one account of a Templar mass in which "a head with a white beard, which had belonged to a former Grand Master'' was set on an altar at midnight and then worshiped by the Templars.

Many researchers have established links between the Knights Templars and the Cathar sect in southern France, a group that was the object of persecution and massacres by papal armies for a thirty-year period in the early 1200s. Even the accounts of their critics report that the Cathars led simple and pious lives. Their ''crime'' was to differ with the Catholic Church in their interpretation of Christ's life on earth. Nor did they accept the crucifixion of Christ. As a result, they were practically exterminated and their properties confiscated.

According to theories linking the Cathars with the Templars, the Cathars possessed some secret treasure or evidence that would shake the foundations of the Catholic Church. This treasure supposedly survived the persecutions and made its way into the hands of the Templars.

Interpretations of this treasure differ greatly. Some say it was an actual physical treasure, others that it was something more mundane but more explosive—such as documents and creeds dating back to the time of Christ. According to Cathar doctrine, the very church that was persecuting *them* as heretics was actually the corrupt organization that had distorted the Gospels and created a material-oriented faith rather than a spiritual one.

But what were these documents or treasures?

The answer is impossible to determine. As with many other ''heretics,'' Cathar books and bibles were burned just as their bodies were, leaving behind a gap through which mystery and supposition rushes in.

An in-depth look at Cathar belief and history can be found in Zoe Oldenbourg's *Massacre at Montsegur*, and one of the best books dealing with possible links between Templar and Cathar thought is *Holy Blood, Holy Grail*, by Michael Baigent, Richard Leigh, and Henry Lincoln.

One of the more obvious connections between Cathar belief and alleged Templar ritual was the Cathar practice of the priest bestowing the kiss of peace upon members of the congregation—a chaste kiss that was often replaced by a touching of hands. Since one of the charges King Philip brought against the Templars was that initiates were the recipients of obscene blasphemous kisses from Templars inducting them into the order, it's easy to see how this idea of "heresy" could be distorted and used against the Templars.

Whatever the teachings of the Cathars were, they found a wide reception in the Languedoc region of France. One of the reasons for this, as stated by Pope Innocent III himself, was the hopelessly corrupt nature of many of his own representatives in the area at the time. The pope singled out bishops, canons, and monks who looted their own dioceses, extorted money from members of their own congregations, and led lives of banditry, sloth, degradation, and sin. With such a record, it's little wonder that the simple and devout practices of the Cathars attracted those looking for spiritual guidance.

Since many of the charges leveled against the Templars mirror Cathar practices, it's possible that King Philip appropriated the "heresies" of the Cathar sect and claimed such practices were rampant in the Knights Templars.

One intriguing connection between the Cathars and the Templars is the subject of the head or idol.

Perhaps the head the Templars were charged with worshiping was one and the same as the one that was formerly in the possession of the Cathars. Speculation about what this head might be has continued for nearly seven hundred years. One of the more interesting theories surfaced a few years ago when British scholar Anthony Harris published his book *The Sacred Virgin and the Holy Whore*. Writing about the book in an article for *Omni* magazine, Ivor Smullen explained Harris's view about Cathar relics listed in records from the Inquisition. Included in the relics was a human skull known as Caput LVIII. Says Smullen: "The Cathari had claimed to possess Christ's flesh and blood, and as far as Harris is concerned, Caput LVIII was the skull." In yet another twist to the story of Head 58, Harris's book suggests that Christ may have been a woman.

Given the political and religious climate of the time, if the Catholic Church believed the Cathars possessed or claimed to possess such relics, it's possible to understand how such relentless Crusades could be waged against the sect deemed heretical by the authorities.

Similarly, if it was believed that the Templars inherited not only the relics but the beliefs of the Cathars, that would put them at odds with the entire Catholic Church. But the Templars claimed all charges against them were false— and that they followed the teachings of Christ.

Arguments for and against the Templars have persisted

over the centuries, but one of the key questions still remains. Did King Philip go to such great lengths to persecute the Templars because of some misguided religious principle of his own? Or was it a much more down-to-earth reason, that the only one worshiping idols was Philip the Fair, who worshiped the heads on the gold and silver coins in the Templar Treasury?

# 4

## Catharsis: The Siege of Montsegur

### The Last Stronghold

Faith can move mountains.

It can also be pushed off a mountain.

That's exactly what happened to the Cathar religion in the year 1243 when the "Crusaders" who'd been pillaging, murdering, raping, and robbing their way through southern France for the past thirty years descended upon the fortress of Montsegur.

Located in the Pyrenees in France's Languedoc region near the Mediterranean coast, Montsegur contained a small number of soldiers who still resisted the predatory hordes from the north of France. But most of the population inside the mountain fortress was made up of civilians, adherents of the Cathar faith, and the priests, or *perfecti*, who were responsible for teaching the austere and devout dogmas of their religion.

Montsegur, at a height of approximately 3,500 feet and

with only one steep hill providing access to the fort, was long considered impregnable. But after decades of laying waste to most of the countryside and sending tens of thousands of innocent people on their way to heaven, the Crusaders had decided upon Montsegur as their ultimate target. It was the center of the Cathar faith and the last major stronghold of resistance to orthodox Christianity.

So the massive army gradually worked its way up the mountain and cut it off from the outside world.

The lord of the castle was Raymond de Perella, a well-respected military man who had provided protection to the Cathars living in the village below the mountain. Rather than yield to the ignoble nobles and the crusading clergymen, Perella threw in his lot with the Cathars and opened his fortress to them.

The attacking army was led by Hugh Des Arcis, who had a force of six to ten thousand French soldiers and mercenaries with him.

There were approximately 150 fighting men inside the castle, most of them knights from the area with strong Cathar connections. The civilians and Cathars accounted for approximately 350 of the defending force.

The defenders held out for nine months, many of them unwilling to even consider surrendering. Ever since Simon de Montfort's earlier Crusaders committed endless atrocities against the Cathar towns—massacring men, women, and children, including fellow Christians as well as alleged heretics—the Cathars had seen little sense in delivering themselves to their enemies.

On several previous occasions, the clergy and Crusaders

had unleashed mercenary bands composed of looters, thieves, and murderers of all kinds on captured populations. They would torture, maim, and murder one and all and make off with whatever plunder they could before the Crusaders came in to steal their portions with the full blessing of the clergymen.

During this period when Christian and heretic alike were massacred, a saying often attributed to Simon de Montfort became quite popular: "Kill Them All, Let God Sort Them Out."

For actions like this the Crusaders were forgiven their past *and present* sins and often gained large holdings from the Cathars.

All in all, these Crusades were one of the most abominable acts ever committed in the name of religion.

And the Cathars in Montsegur knew full well their likely fate if they surrendered without negotiating acceptable terms for the defenders.

## Defenders of the Faith(s)

The Cathar faith, which was deemed heretical by Pope Innocent III, had become widespread in the Languedoc region, mainly because many of the bishops and priests in the area had become so corrupt that even the pope had to condemn their actions. Since some of the pope's own representatives had become involved in widespread cases of looting, debauchery, and assassination, the common people looked elsewhere for religious guidance.

They found it in the Cathar faith, which maintained that *it* had kept alive the true teachings of Christianity and that the organized church was corrupt. The Cathars practiced poverty, chastity, and communal responsibility. They also believed that it was the responsibility of each of their followers to establish a personal relationship with God that could come about only through prayer, meditation, and good works.

In short, the Cathars followed most of the same practices that were advocated by the established church. They differed in a number of respects, however.

Like the Arian Christians of the early fourth century whose teachings were eventually purged from orthodox Christianity, the Cathars believed that Christ was a prophet who showed the way to God. They didn't believe in the Trinity.

Like many of the Templars, the Cathars didn't worship the Cross or the Crucifixion, believing that it represented the evil that was done to Christ on earth. Another reason the Cathars were seen as a threat to the established church was their belief that priests weren't meant to be a caste set apart from the rest of the believers, and, in fact, that everyone, men and women alike, should aspire to become perfecti themselves.

To the Cathars the established church was corrupt, and to the established church the Cathars were corrupt. Both began referring to the other as the "Synagogue of Satan."

Aside from the religious differences, there were also political and monetary considerations involved. The Cathar lands in the south of France were rich and prosperous and ripe for the plucking. The northern French saw a chance to increase their lands as the pope sought to increase the influence of the Church in the area.

And so the Cathars were sacrificed on the altar of religion.

## The Fall of the Fortress

After nine months of holding off the siege on Montsegur, Raymond de Perella realized that eventually the fortress would be overrun. The Crusaders had inched forward over the months, launching small skirmishes that gradually won them the outer defenses of the fortress.

With catapults and battering rams, as well as several thousand more troops on their side, the Crusaders were certain of victory.

The Cathars agreed to surrender—but only after a lengthy negotiation of terms. According to this agreement, the soldiers would be able to walk away from the fortress and so would the civilians. In fact, any of the "heretics" who renounced their faith and converted to orthodox Christianity could also leave Montsegur unharmed. Those who persisted in their Cathar faith would share the fate of many a heretic before them: they would be burned at the stake.

These relatively benevolent terms were accepted by many of the civilians and most of the soldiers. But instead of walking away from certain death, a good number of the soldiers converted to Catharism.

Nearly three hundred people went free. However, almost two hundred Cathars accepted their fate when the Crusaders and Inquisitors led them from the fortress and roped them into a wooden enclosure to be burned at the stake en masse.

Under the eyes of the Inquisition, the burning began. It lasted for hours, scorching the air with the sacrificed souls of the Cathars.

At least four of the perfecti escaped their fate, since they had been designated to carry away the treasure of the Cathars. Scaling down the cliff side of the mountain on long ropes, Amiel Aicart and three others avoided the flames.

As mentioned in the earlier chapter on the Templars, the treasure they removed from Montsegur was believed to have been the Holy Grail and perhaps some secret gospels or documents that were the basis of their faith. Some writers have guessed that this "treasure" of the Cathars was the sole reason the Crusades were launched in the first place.

But the treasure, like many of the Cathars, would soon be relegated to the lost pages of history.

## From Out of the Fire

While the Cathars were eventually subdued by the decades-long Crusades waged against them, Cathar beliefs surfaced periodically over the centuries.

In the 1970s, reports of some modern-day "Cathars"

surfaced thanks to the work of Arthur Guirdham, a psychiatrist in England who encountered a troubled woman who came to him for treatment. Her story seemed incredibly bizarre at first, since it involved horrifying memories of a previous incarnation—as a Cathar who was burned as a heretic.

Guirdham investigated the revelations of the woman and, after checking out many of the details, accepted her story. From there his investigations spiraled, until eventually he uncovered a small group of people who were believed to be living in the present day as reincarnated Cathars.

In 1970 and 1974, Guirdham wrote two books on the subject, *The Cathars and Reincarnation* and *We Are One Another*, both published by Neville Spearman in London.

# 5

## Martyrs, Madmen, and Messiahs

From the beginning of time, messianic leaders have appeared out of the blue, struck by sudden visions or guided by celestial voices or apparitions that transformed their lives. Many times these visions also changed the shape of the world around them, causing great spiritual and nationalist movements.

Other times these martyrs and messiahs had a short-term effect on their world, like shooting stars that blazed across the landscape with incendiary effect.

Some of these leaders were saints. Some of them were sinners.

But all of them had one thing in common: for a short time on earth they were touched by madness—and sometimes greatness.

This chapter looks at some of these visions and visionaries.

## Joan of Arc: The Warrior Child

Joan of Arc was thirteen years old when she first heard the voice of an angel in the garden of her family home in the small village of Domrémy, France.

It was a time when people found it easier to believe in miracles—and a time when miracles were needed.

The country we now know as France was a collection of small kingdoms at the time of Joan of Arc. Some were loyal to the King of France, some to the Duke of Burgundy. Some of them even considered themselves Englishmen, because of family ties to the warlike British who often raided and plundered France. Still others were loyal to whatever army happened to be pillaging the area at the time.

Whomever they were loyal to, the nobles of the region were often involved in feuds and small wars of their own that always seemed to drag in the common people.

At first the wars seemed distant to Joan. She was a peasant girl whose main task was to tend the cows of the village with the other children. Aside from the normal play with other children her age, Joan's main activity seemed to be praying.

Joan wanted to have a normal life. So when voices and visions came to her in the garden she was awed, but not interested. Even when the apparition identified itself as Saint Michael the Archangel—who wanted her to take up arms and lead the French against the English—she tried to resist the celestial commands.

Even though the apparitions began appearing with greater frequency and urgency, Joan dismissed them and tried to go on about her life.

But then the voices came back. So did the visions. They called out to her and dared her to take up arms in the name of God and drive the British from the land.

Still Joan demurred. The idea of a child—a girl, no less—assuming command of the French armies seemed too absurd to consider.

But the bright luminous clouds returned again and again, slowly taking shape before her eyes. St. Michael. St. Catherine. The pantheon of saints worked upon her with their endless appearances. They always had the same message: she must lead the armies of God against the occupying armies laying waste to the land.

Eventually, after consulting with the local priest and praying to God for guidance, Joan answered the call.

The seventeen-year-old girl went to Chinon and convinced the Dauphin—the uncrowned king of France—of the truth of her visions by telling him things that only he could know.

She had previously convinced one of his captains by telling him of events happening hundreds of miles away—events that were proved true weeks later when word of the battle she described in her vision reached the captain.

The Dauphin sent her on to Orléans, where her presence miraculously transformed a lackluster group of soldiers into a band of almost invincible warriors who

followed her into battle against the English who had besieged the town.

Angels were on the battlefield.

Celestial voices were in the air.

Visions were descending upon her and her followers
one after the other, visions that led to victory. The British,
who'd proved unbeatable for months, had to flee before
the Maid of Orléans.

It had become a holy war now. Against all odds, the
Maid of Orléans went on to lead the French armies to
several other victories. Her record of victories against the
English was so overwhelming that they were convinced
she was a witch or a sorceress.

Everything the celestial voices told her came to pass.

She raised the siege of Orléans.

She saw the Dauphin crowned king.

She drove the English out of most of the French territory
over which they'd taken control.

But, unfortunately, other prophecies also came true.
The visions told her that she would be betrayed, captured,
and killed. Her celestial visitors even told her the hour
of her death. Almost as if she were a sacrificial soldier
playing out a heavenly role on earth, she found herself
living a future that had been shown to her by her celestial
advisers.

The king abandoned her in her hour of need and the
British troops caught her. In a fixed trial that condemned
her as a witch, she was burned on the stake—just as the
angels had predicted. Just as she had told the world.

\* \* \*

All those who were close to Joan of Arc testified to the miraculous events that seemed to follow her wherever she went. Healings. Prophecies. Victories. The locations of great relics, including the Sword of Fierbois, were revealed to her in dreams that invariably came true.

But as time passed—and the memory of her martyrdom on the stake began to fade—people began to question the reality of what had happened. Had angels really descended to counsel her? Had they spoken in tongues only she could hear? Or were these just visions and voices from within her own mind that were guiding her?

In the years to come, some factions would denounce her as a liar, a madwoman, or a witch. Others would pronounce her a saint and savior of her country.

But whatever side of the argument is taken, one thing remains true: her visions did change the history of France and perhaps the world.

## Brazilian Messiahs

The region around Bahia in the northern part of Brazil is considered by many to be a modern-day Paradise. The land on the Atlantic coastline is a strip of golden beaches. Farther into the interior, the land is rich with forest.

For a while during the years 1895 to 1897, a Brazilian messiah named Antonio Conselheiro tried to make this a literal paradise on earth. The Counselor, or, as he was also called, Bom Jesus, brought his messianic movement to a large ranch known as Canudos.

Conselheiro claimed he'd been selected to pave the way for the Second Coming of Christ, which would happen in his holy land of Canudos.

His dogma attracted disciples who believed in free love and a freewheeling lifestyle. But rather than turn the other cheek, his followers were quite familiar with weapons of all kinds and used them regularly to keep their paradise unspoiled by the forces of the outside world.

Conselheiro was a guerrilla guru with a lot of charisma and eccentric ideas about heavenly hygiene. As mentioned in Donald E. Worcester's 1973 book *Brazil, From Colony to World Power*, "He neither bathed nor combed for years, and as his holy influence extended farther and farther about him, the number of his faithful followers increased." Many of these followers were militant disciples with criminal records who continued their thieving ways with a frightening fervor.

When Prudente de Morais, the first president of the Brazilian republic, responded to calls from the public to rid the countryside of this sacred thorn in their side, he sent in police and militia to remove the messiah.

But Conselheiro's people met the expedition with armed resistance. And with God on their side, they won. At least that was the interpretation of many of the people who fought against him.

In their fascinating collection of millennialist movements, *A History of the End of the World*, Yuri Rubinsky and Ian Wiseman mention the outcome of a second expedition that was sent against Bom Jesus. ''. . . but just at the end of the battle, a stray bullet killed the colonel who led the expedition. His soldiers fled in panic and disarray, believing they were in the presence of supernatural forces.''

After a number of additional skirmishes in which thousands of the messiah's followers defeated all forces sent to subdue them, the army responded in force, descending upon Canudos and, with a great loss of life on both sides, destroying the movement and the messiah.

But as a look at a map of Brazil shows today, the messiah was not forgotten, as evidenced by the backcountry place named Bom Jesus da Lapa.

The messianic movement didn't end with the death of Conselheiro. A priest named Padre Cicero Romão Batista started a similar movement that combined political goals with the religious realm, once again forming a guerrilla force for God.

But one of the most well-known spiritual descendants of Bom Jesus was João Maria the Monk, who had received his enlightenment at the hands of Antonio Conselheiro.

João Maria, claiming that he had been passed the baton by Conselheiro, began a similar campaign that attracted the wild-eyed and the wicked, who flocked to the Contestado region of Brazil. It was a Wild West–like area controlled by João Maria's metaphysical and martial force.

Before he could usher in the Second Coming, the military struck in force, sending in an army of six thousand men who brought about a personal Apocalypse for João Maria's followers in 1915.

## Military Messiahs

While many of the messianic figures who earned a place in history took up the gauntlet in order to preserve their faith from attack, a number of these messiahs were military men to begin with. For them the religious aspect seemed secondary and was, in many cases, grafted onto them by their followers or cultivated as a subtle form of propaganda.

The early-fourth-century emperor Constantine owed his conquest and unification of the Roman Empire to his "visions" of a cross in the sky. Using this divine revelation as a symbol to unite Christians beneath his banner, he took Rome from Maxentius and solidified his hold on the empire.

But, according to the histories of Constantine, he was actually a pagan warrior whose "Christian" beliefs leaned toward the so-called Arian heresy. Despite his tolerance and shaping of Christianity, he actually considered himself a divinity.

Another military messiah can be found in the Spanish warrior known as El Cid, who died in the year 1099 after an amazing career as a warlord and ruler.

Because of his great victories against Arab armies, numerous reports of miracles materialized after his victories.

Angelic hordes were seen riding with his troops, and saints hovering above the battlefield.

Despite the messianic myths attached to him, El Cid was a great military leader who fought on both sides during the "religious" struggles—for Arab armies as well as Christian. But like many other larger-than-life military men who left their mark on history, he was seen as a divinely inspired champion whose victories often were attributed to a warlike god looking down from above.

# 6

# Lunatic Legions

When the Inquisition was officially created at the beginning of the thirteenth century, it was supposed to be an instrument of the church to stamp out heresy, witchcraft, and other evils plaguing all of Europe. By the time it ended hundreds of years later, with its last echoes of insanity playing out in Salem, Massachusetts, the Inquisition itself had become so evil and corrupt that many of the priests and monks charged with enforcing it raised their voices against it.

By then the officers of the Inquisition had proved beyond doubt that there was indeed evil plaguing the land—in the form of the Inquisitors themselves, who'd practiced every form of torture known to man. They destroyed human bodies and souls on the rack, at the stake, by crushing with rocks, and by any means imaginable that came to their tortured minds.

In many cases—as seen by the wars waged against the Cathars—the Inquisition had become a tool for genocide.

It had also become a tool for anyone who wanted revenge against any enemy, or a chance to take over property. Simply claiming someone was a witch was enough to have that person convicted. There was no defense. Under torture, the accused would say anything the Inquisitors wanted them to say, manufacturing stories about other witches and heretics. This gave the Inquisitors an ever-increasing list of the "guilty" with which to work.

In this manner hundreds of thousands of innocent people were murdered, tortured, hanged, and burned at the stake, often on the word of jealous neighbors or witch-finders who traveled across Europe collecting fees for every witch they found. With money as an incentive, it was only natural they found witches wherever they looked.

But aside from the hysteria and contagion of intolerance and madness that made life a horror for individuals accused of heresy, there were several instances of organized purges against entire populations. As seen in the following examples, often the only thing these people were guilty of was their belief in freedom and the dignity of the human spirit.

## The Stedinger "Heretics"

A political struggle in Germany between an archbishop of Bremen and a people known as Stedingers erupted into a "heretical" uprising that resulted in the formation of a lunatic legion—an army of forty thousand soldiers that was raised on the command of Pope Gregory IX.

This army was sent in to exterminate the people of

Steding for alleged crimes that are too ludicrous for a sane person to give credence to. But at the time, these charges provided a good excuse to crush the Stedingers, who had managed to create a small democracy-like territory of their own and had maintained their independence for years.

The Archbishop of Bremen and the Count of Oldenburg had designs on their land, however, and systematically began encroaching upon their territory until, finally, armed conflict broke out. The Stedingers fought against the hordes of freebooters, mercenaries, thieves, and criminals of all kinds their enemies sent against them.

Responding to the archbishop's plea for assistance, Pope Gregory IX declared the Stedingers to be heretics. It was now open season on them, and anyone who raided their land to rid it of heretics would be considered a devout Christian soldier.

The devout soldiers began massacring men, women, and children on a massive scale—but the Stedingers managed to win several great victories against the Count of Oldenburg. It appeared for a while that the Stedingers had actually won their freedom.

But the Crusade was just starting.

Along with the usual crimes of using witchery and sorcery to make cows stop giving milk and causing crops to fail, the Stedingers were now accused of all forms of bizarre devil worship.

In a letter sent out to the bishops all across Europe in order to arouse them into forming a much larger army of crusaders, Gregory IX wrote about the regular appearance of the devil at the ceremonies of the Stedingers. Included in the letter is a statement so bizarre as to be laughable, but under the prevailing climate of intolerance, it too was added to the list of Stedinger atrocities: "The devil appears to them in different shapes—sometimes as a goose or a duck . . ." With plenty of fowl in the area, it was believed by some that the entire region was infested by demonic ducks.

But such strange flights of fancy were enough to indict the Stedingers.

The Archbishop of Mainz responded to the pope's call for a Crusade. Along with many nobles with designs on the region, an army numbering nearly forty thousand troops was amassed. Under the banner of the Duke of Brabant, they marched into Stedinger territory.

In a last gasp of resistance, the Stedingers raised an army of their own to fight the invaders. But they were hopelessly outnumbered. An army of eight thousand Stedingers was destroyed, and the civilian population was put to the sword. The rich farmlands and forests were then torched—with righteously induced hellfire.

## The Holy Hermit

An even earlier lunatic legion was formed during the years of the First Crusade when huge armies were formed in Europe and sent to do battle for the Holy Land.

This legion was formed by a charismatic—and perhaps insane—man known as Peter the Hermit, whose preachings attracted thousands of followers who traveled with him from country to country. His grand plan was to take them to Jerusalem to drive the Turks from the Holy Land.

Peter the Hermit's Crusade was inspired by an earlier trip to Jerusalem during which he claimed Christ had appeared to him in a vision. After convincing Pope Urban II of the authenticity of his vision, he began the call for a Crusade.

With the pope's backing, he was successful in raising a huge "army" from France, Germany, and Italy. This army was made up of authentic pilgrims, as well as criminals, prostitutes, monks, soldiers, beggars, and fanatics.

Peter the Hermit led them to the Holy Land to fight the infidel and stamp out heretics wherever they found them. Unfortunately, many of these Crusaders had no conception of what a heretic or an infidel was, but they knew they had to be around somewhere.

As a result the Crusaders began fighting even before they left Europe, descending like locusts upon the Hungarian and Bulgarian countryside. They began killing "infidels," who, according to their developing philosophy, were any people who happened to be in their way and spoke a different language. They stormed cities throughout Europe, massacring the inhabitants and plundering the countryside as part of their holy calling.

The kings of Hungary and Bulgaria finally drove the errant Crusaders out of their land, sending many of them to heaven at the point of a sword.

When the ravenous horde reached Constantinople, the base of operations for launching Crusaders into the Holy Land, the rabble began plundering Constantinople itself.

Finally they moved on toward the Holy Land, only to be destroyed en route by their first encounter with a Turkish army. Peter the Hermit stayed behind to receive more visions and provide his divine counsel to the next round of Crusaders en route to the Holy Land.

## Torquemada

The inequities of the Inquisition reached their height under the stewardship of Tomás de Torquemada, who became the Grand Inquisitor in 1452.

From his sanctuary in Spain, Torquemada initiated a reign of holy terror so dreadful in its carnage and destruction of the human spirit that his name still brings a shudder today.

With the blessing of Pope Sixtus IV, Torquemada went about ridding the land of heretics. And, as with most Inquisitors, he found them everywhere. Men, women, peasants, nobles, all of them fell under the watchful eye of Torquemada.

They were put to the rack.

They were clubbed.

They were burned.

They were slashed with whips.

They were hanged.

All in the search for evil.

Thousands of the accused went to their deaths on little more than a whispered accusation.

Their property was confiscated by the Church.

And the Inquisition rolled on.

After a long and bloody reign, with many of the clergy and nobles of the time trying to get him ousted from his position, Torquemada passed on the baton to other Inquisitors and went off to a monastery to reflect on all the good he had done.

## The End of the Insanity

Although much of the hysterical persecution caused by the Inquisition and the crusading armies was carried out under the auspices of the Church, in many cases it was the clergy who finally brought about the end of this insanity.

Priests all across Europe stood up to denounce the Inquisition—resulting in many of them being put to death as heretics. Eventually, after entire populations of innocent people were killed in the most hideous ways possible, the arguments of the rational clergy and nobles brought the Inquisitors to their senses.

The Inquisition gradually lost its power—its moral charter as empty as the charges it had leveled against the "heretics" it sought to destroy.

# 7

# Vampire General

## The Horrifying Hero of Romania

The fanged creature of the night created by Bram Stoker in 1897 was but a deathly pale shadow of the real Dracula—or, as he was more frequently known, Vlad the Impaler. Throughout history he's been known under several other names, including Vlad Tepes, Son of the Dragon, and Son of the Devil.

No doubt the poor victims who fell under his control called him an even greater variety of names. Aside from waging endless war to maintain the sovereignty of his country, Dracula seemed to devote his life to creating a hell on earth for anyone who displeased him, friend or foe, wife or lover. His wrath could turn on anyone, and no one in his homeland was safe.

In many ways he was a demonic serial killer. He had tens of thousands of people put to death by impalement on wooden stakes, or by strangulation, mutilation, burning, and whatever other gruesome embellishments came to mind. Add to this the number of deaths caused during warfare, and his body count dwarfs anything dreamed up by a fiction writer.

Bram Stoker's literary creation *Dracula* came to him during a dream—at least, that is how the story goes. But he also borrowed heavily from Transylvanian history and the rugged geography of the Carpathian Mountains. From this historical seed Bram Stoker went about planting the images of the cloaked count and his ravishing retinue in the minds of his Victorian readers.

Since that first appearance in England, the novel *Dracula* has been widely translated and transformed in adaptations and imitations on screen and in print. And still the tale is resurrected time and time again on stage and screen and in new editions of the novel.

While Stoker's novel won international fame, so did the real-life accounts of Vlad the Impaler. His horrible deeds and warlike ways were captured in many pamphlets and broadsides that appeared shortly after his death.

Originating with the boyars and burghers who were most victimized by Dracula, these accounts soon gained a wide circulation across Europe. Portraits and woodcuts from that time portray him as a wide-eyed, regal presence whose stare could be as effective as the hypnotic Evil Eye that many people at the time believed in.

Though the pamphlets made him out to be a monster, Dracula probably would have enjoyed seeing them were he alive. And perhaps he would have authored a few of his own, adding even more horrifying details.

He was a master of psychological warfare, which he waged relentlessly against his enemies. He wanted the name Dracula to be a name to be reckoned with, a name to give nightmares to even the most brutal foe.

With the knowledge of the gruesome fate that would befall them if they ever fell into his hands, many of the most aggressive warriors stepped slowly in Transylvania.

## The Making of a Monster

Dracula was born in the year 1431 in the Transylvanian province of Sighişoara, a site that recently came into prominence during the revolt against modern-day tyrant Nicolai Ceauşescu, whose draconian reign finally came to an end in 1989 when the Romanian people rose up against him and his Securitate secret police.

More than five hundred years ago, Dracula inspired similar feelings among his countrymen. Some of them hated him with a passion, considering him the most evil ruler on the face of the earth. Others looked to him as a hero who held their country together and protected it against Turkish invaders.

Both sides were right in their own way. Dracula was a heroic figure when it came to military matters. But he was also a monster when it came to ruling his own people.

Dracula's kingdom was based in the province of Wallachia in what is now Romania. It was the same troubled realm that was ruled by his father, a warlord known as Vlad Dracul, a member of the Order of the Dragon, a chivalrous Christian order established to fight the so-called "infidel" hordes that threatened to sweep across Europe.

Vlad Dracul managed to survive in a world of shifting alliances, sometimes throwing in his lot with Turks, other times representing the crumbling Holy Roman Empire as a devout knight. Throughout his reign Vlad Dracul lived the life of a warrior. Regardless of the side he fought on, he was considered an honorable man—but perhaps not by the famed Hungarian leader Hunyadi, who eventually killed him for not coming to his side in times of trouble.

As the son of Dracul, Vlad Tepes was called Dracula. He inherited the same unsteady fate as Vlad Dracul, having to seize the throne from his Christian rivals while he was backed by the Turks. This strange situation came about because Vlad Dracul was forced to deliver his two sons, Dracula and Radu, to the Turks as hostages while he was allied with them.

Brutalized by the Turks during his younger years, Dracula cultivated a hatred toward them that would bear strange fruit in years to come when thousands of his Turkish captives died agonizing deaths on the tall stakes, their limbs writhing like bloodied vines.

Death by impalement was but one of the techniques he learned from the Turks when he was a hostage. Dracula refined the practice by using blunter-edged poles to impale his victims so they would live longer and suffer more before they died. His victims were impaled in every way imaginable; he often created grotesque living and writhing sculptures like an inhuman artist.

On some occasions Dracula put entire villages of his own people to death in this manner. Other times he reserved the impalement for captured soldiers. But no one could be sure if they were friend or enemy, because the slightest provocation could turn Dracula against them.

Aside from the torture methods, Dracula gained a detailed knowledge of Turkish military tactics, which he used to great advantage in his wars against the Turks.

But the initial seizure of the throne was made possible only by the backing of the Turks, who wanted to install what they considered a "friend" on the Wallachian throne. And Dracula was a friend and ally to them, at least until he considered himself strong enough to take part in the Crusades against them.

## The Dragon Awakes

Despite his well-deserved reputation for inhuman cruelty, at times Dracula was considered the last best hope of Christianity. His kingdom was right on the edge of the Western empire, the crossroads between the Christian West and the Muslim East.

Dracula's realm was a gateway to the rest of Europe for the encroaching Turkish forces. If Wallachia fell to the Turks, soon the advance armies of the Ottoman Empire would begin swallowing the kingdoms farther to the west.

While the kings of Hungary, Germany, and Moldavia were hypothetically launching holy Crusades against the

Turks, in reality they often stayed in their own kingdoms, where they were involved in feuds of their own. This left Dracula as the guardian of the border.

Because of Dracula's own resistance against the Turks, he received the backing and support of Pope Pius II, who, like Dracula, was able to be flexible when it came to matters of survival.

Though he may have been considered a champion of the Christian empire, in reality the prince of Wallachia was a nomadic warlord. Of necessity he constantly moved his relatively small forces from stronghold to stronghold in order to survive invasions by much larger armies.

At times, when he could marshal up to thirty thousand troops, his army was large enough to confront invaders on the battlefield. But most of the time Dracula was embattled within his own country as the boyars of the ruling class sought to undermine his rule. Since they were the premier targets of his wrath, it's quite understandable that they didn't want to see a strong Dracula on the throne. But at the same time, because of their chaotic support and mercenary interests, Dracula was always ready to persecute them for what he perceived as disloyalty to the country.

## Let Sleeping Vampires Lie

Like many other medieval leaders (Charlemagne, Arthur, and El Cid, for example) who were believed to be "undead" and biding their time to return at the country's hour of greatest need, Dracula was also considered to be one of those temporary exiles from this world.

But because of his well-known penchant for impaling people, the potential return of Dracula was dreaded by many of those who had survived his wars and his wrath. This fear was illuminated and exaggerated by the historical—and hysterical—pamphlets circulated by the Transylvanian boyars and burghers who were the main target of his purges.

Another reason why Dracula was believed to be alive was simply a result of the dissemination of news in those days. Word of battles or catastrophes often took an incredibly long amount of time to travel from country to country, and the "facts" often became greatly distorted. News of Dracula's decapitation could transform into his deification by the time the story came to rest.

There was also the matter of propaganda by his enemies *and* his allies, who repeatedly promised troops for the Crusade against the Turks but never actually left their own kingdoms. What better excuse for their inaction than to portray Vlad Dracula as an inhuman and treacherous monster? Better to keep the troops home than to risk their destruction at the hands of such a tyrant.

When Dracula finally was resurrected—in Stoker's 1897 novel—he was cloaked in gothic trappings and given supernatural abilities that, if the original Dracula possessed, he certainly would have used to evade his pursuers.

Stoker's Dracula could discorporate into a mist or travel in the form of a luminous cloud. He could also demonically transform himself into the shape of animals to prowl the countryside. In the novel, rather than using the stairs, Dracula had a lizardlike habit of inching down the casement walls of his castle or flying away in the form of a bat.

But the real-life Dracula was often trapped in castles built high on Carpathian passes, with no exit but his own ferocious martial skills.

Although Dracula was a brutal despot, he was also capable of rewarding and bestowing honors upon those who served his cause—regardless of their origin.

This was yet another sore point for the upper classes, who found themselves toppled from their lofty positions and replaced by commoners who had proved their bravery in battle time and again—while the boyars sat safely in their well-appointed homes.

With this new class of capable fighting men, Dracula was able to fashion a military force of daring soldiers he felt kinship with. Naturally, this increased the animosity between the boyars and their prince.

Consequently, when times were good and Dracula's victories won him renown across the land, the boyars were reluctantly supportive. But when Dracula's fortunes were reversed and he was forced to retreat from his enemies in fear for his life, many of the boyars eagerly supported his pursuers.

Faced with conspiracy against his throne from within the kingdom and without, Dracula's reign was interrupted several times. On occasion he was toppled from his throne by superior forces of Turks. One of his perennial enemies was his brother Radu, who seized the throne with the backing of his Turkish allies.

Dracula also spent more than a decade as a "prisoner" of *his* Christian allies, who kept him off the throne and out of trouble. But the Wallachian warlord was eventually released from prison when another crusade was launched against the Turks and it was realized that Dracula would be one of the greatest generals to send against his lifelong enemies.

By marching off to war, Dracula was able to restore his reputation and install himself on the throne once again.

## Blood Royale

Dracula was the victim of bad press in one regard—the drinking of blood. There's little evidence to support the numerous stories that he drank blood to satisfy vampirish needs. He *was* bloodthirsty, as just about any history of the period will reveal.

The reason Dracula is often accused of being a vampire stems from an episode in which he put an entire town to death by impalement and then dined in their midst to enjoy the sound of their death throes—a hideous real-life antecedent of Grand Guignol dinner theater.

This incident also started rumors that Dracula engaged in cannibalism, but it seems the cannibalism connected to his court were cases of torture where he forced other people to engage in the practice, sometimes having them eat members of their own family. However, these tales of cannibalism and blood drinking are almost incidental to his greater cruelties.

Impalement was not the only form of torture exacted upon his enemies and those unfortunates he decided were criminals or criminally insolent. After a diplomatic conference at his castle, for example, Dracula had his soldiers nail the turbans of Turkish envoys onto their heads because they hadn't removed them while in his presence.

Likewise, Dracula was capable of inhuman innovation when it came to cleansing his lands of outlaws or the poor and the sick. To solve the problem of those who wandered hungry through the countryside, he invited them all to a great feast and served them a meal fit for a king.

Unfortunately for them, this proved to be their last meal. When the feast was over, he sealed them inside a hall and set it aflame, burning them to death.

In spite of all of these gruesome practices, in some ways Dracula was a devout man. He had a puritan attitude toward sexual conduct—of others, at least—and enforced it with a deadly efficiency. You were either prim and proper in his presence or you were dead. You were a law-abiding citizen or you were reduced to ashes. He tolerated no variations from his creed of conduct.

## The Wallachian Warlord

Even though the death toll was high from those occasions when Dracula put entire towns to the sword or stake, almost as much blood was shed during the battles that Dracula fought.

By necessity a master of guerrilla warfare, Dracula would harass invading armies with sudden hit-and-run cavalry attacks or ambush them with archers hidden in the thick Romanian forests. Then he would vanish, leaving behind the panic-stricken invaders alone with their dead.

While the Turks—and sometimes the armies of his former Christian allies—often were able to capture the castles on the borders of his territory, by the time they moved to the rugged interior of his province, their armies would be spread out or holed up in temporary encampments, providing Dracula with more targets to overwhelm.

Dracula was a skilled soldier who channeled his rage onto the battlefield, personally leading his men into battle. He waded deep into enemy ranks with a fearless abandon that inspired his troops to follow suit.

One well-known foray established his reputation among the people of his own country as well as among the invading Turks. When a Turkish host of sixty thousand or more soldiers moved deep into his country, Dracula gathered a small force of shock troops and under cover of darkness rode right into their camp. The Turks suddenly found themselves falling under the swords of nearly two thousand Wallachian warriors attacking them from the middle of their camp. The leader of the Turks narrowly avoided capture before Dracula led his people back into the darkness.

From then on, no one underestimated the daring of Dracula.

When the Turks moved even farther into the heart of Dracula's empire, they were in for even greater shocks. For, as they neared his stronghold, they encountered thousands upon thousands of Turkish corpses impaled all through the countryside like signposts on the road to hell.

## The Death of Dracula and the Birth of a Legend

Dracula was finally killed near Bucharest, which he'd fortified as his capital shortly before he had to abandon it from overwhelming enemy forces. But there is some argument over whether he was killed by one of his own people, by soldiers under the command of his brother Radu, or by Turks.

It occurred in a small skirmish—small because at the end Dracula had only a tiny core of troops who remained loyal to him.

Dracula was beheaded and his corpse was allegedly taken to the island monastery of Snagov, where he had long provided a sanctuary for monks. His burial at this island Avalon was considered to be a rumor at first, but over the years a considerable amount of evidence pointed toward it as indeed being the vampire general's final resting place.

Snagov has remained a popular tourist attraction to this day—high on the list of those who wish to take one of the tours that explore sites that Dracula actually inhabited.

At Snagov a princely tomb was unearthed by the Romanian government in 1931. But it was only possible to make a probable rather than positive identification. For the corpse buried there had been reduced to a fine skeletal dust—perhaps light enough for an ''undead'' Dracula to fly away in the mist circling the romantic ruins of Snagov.

# 8

## Cryptic Columbus

### The Knight of Christ

Bright red crosses appeared on the horizon, emblazoned on the white sails billowing in the trade winds that carried the *Niña*, *Pinta*, and *Santa María* toward the New World on October 12, 1492. Commanding this singular expedition from the deck of the *Santa María* was a newly titled "Admiral of the Ocean Seas" obsessed with the idea of expanding the kingdom of Spain for Queen Isabella and King Ferdinand.

But he also carried the banner for an otherworldly kingdom. For Christopher Columbus believed he was a cosmic messenger preordained by fate to bring about the Apocalypse. He considered himself "the bearer of Christ," as his frequent signature *Christum ferens* indicated. It was up to him to set the earthly stage for the Second Coming.

For more than a decade this half-mad mariner would sail upon the seas of religious ecstasy, bumping into the

West Indies and the tip of the South American continent before his hopes and dreams were finally dashed forever on the shores of doubt and delusion. Convinced he'd found the Garden of Eden on earth and perhaps the legendary site of King Solomon's Mines, Columbus could never understand why the monarchs he risked his life for didn't fulfill the last prophecy he set for himself. He questioned why the kings and queens of Europe couldn't see that his voyages of discovery were all part of God's plan—a plan meant to culminate with Christopher Columbus riding triumphantly through the gates of Jerusalem at the head of a Christian horde assembled from all corners of the world.

Though he perceived that he failed his cosmic mission, in a way Columbus *did* bring about the end of the world— at least the end of the world the natives of America once knew. His messianic voyages brought Europe and America together for richer and poorer in a marriage that gave birth to a new world.

Gold was on his mind when Columbus first set sail from the Canary Islands off the west coast of Africa with three ships and ninety men who would change the course of history. But the incessant hunger for gold was only a means to an end. After all, Crusades didn't come cheap. According to the terms Columbus demanded from the king and queen, he would receive ten percent of all that he discovered. That tithe could fund a Crusade only if he found a golden hoard of undreamt-of riches.

Thirty-three days after they sailed off into the unknown, the Admiral's three ships landed in the New World, thinking they'd made contact with the farthest reaches of the Old World. Columbus was expecting to see the fabled kingdoms of Japan, China, and India, the treasure-filled lands written about by Marco Polo and other explorers.

Instead he found isolated islands with palm trees and dangerous reefs. And the natives who encountered Columbus shortly after his landing were not Asians bedecked in finery. Nor did they appear to have much gold on them. They were half-naked Arawaks, peaceful "Indians" curious about the light-skinned strangers who'd come to their land in such strange crafts.

And so the Admiral and his people went out among the natives on the island Columbus would name San Salvador, eager to learn their language, convert them to Christianity—and find out where they kept their gold.

The natives began to wonder if these people from across the sea were gods or devils.

Both guesses would subsequently prove right. The treatment of the Caribbean and South American natives by the men on board these three ships and the countless others to come after them would vary in tragic degree.

Some of the European explorers and colonists would look upon the natives as childlike innocents whose measure of humanity would be determined by whether or not they could be converted to Christianity. Others would look upon them as a convenient supply of slaves to be worked to death in the gold and silver mines or the cane fields—or, if they were women, turned into concubines and servants for their own private harems.

According to the Dominican monk Bartolemé de Las

Casas, a contemporary of Columbus who, in his *History of the Indies*, recorded atrocities committed by the colonists, some of the Indians were used as little more than live targets for the colonists to practice their sword work upon. In one passage from his book, the monk writes of how little value the explorers placed on the lives of the natives. "Two of these so-called Christians met two Indian boys one day, each carrying a parrot; they took the parrots and for fun beheaded the boys." Another passage explains how colonists recruited their help: "There were two kinds of servants. One, all the boys and girls taken from their parents on their plundering and killing expeditions, whom they kept in the house night and day . . . And two, seasonal workers for the mines and the fields, who returned to their own homes starving, exhausted, and debilitated."

## Columbus Unchained

Though Columbus is not considered a cruel man for his time, the suffering of native populations apparently meant little to him, as evidenced by the number of Indians he brought back to Spain after his first voyage, like so many human souvenirs. In his own journal entries he wrote about how easily the Indians could be taken for slaves or killed off by a relatively small force of trained soldiers. In fact, one of the reasons he was brought back to Spain in chains after his third voyage to the Indies were the outrages committed against the natives he governed. Under his stewardship murder, rape, robbery, and slavery had reached epidemic proportions, spurred on by the colonists' endless search for gold and converts to the Christian faith. When Isabella and Ferdinand heard of the loathsome treatment of natives typical under his rule, they ordered him arrested and brought back home to face charges.

Columbus was actually put in chains like a common criminal when he was sent back to Spain. Though he could have made the journey without wearing the chains, he chose to keep the chains on him until he could appear before the king and queen.

This dramatic return of the martyr had its desired effect. Horrified by the sight of the Admiral in his pitiful chains, the monarchs forgave him and *almost* restored him to his exalted position. But from then on Columbus was a liability to them. Though he was allowed to make a fourth voyage to the Indies, he was forbidden to stop at some of the lands he'd discovered. They were under new management.

Concerned with losing face and the large fortune promised him, Columbus plunged even deeper into the mystical, becoming a melancholy messiah who donned the robes of Franciscan monks and walked through Spanish streets like a penitent. He also brought forth into the world his *Book of Prophecies*, which clearly pointed to him as the man chosen by God to bear the cross and regain the Holy City. Along with the physical chains, the restraints that once played down his messianic claims were also thrown off.

Though this recall of the Admiral at first appears to be a matter of conscience on the part of the king and queen, it seems more like a case of selective punishment. The harsh treatment Columbus and his men meted out to the natives of the New World would later be surpassed by the conquistadors who ranged all over South and Central America.

The Spaniards were not alone in the subjugation of the continent. The navies of other European countries soon sent out their own explorers—as well as privateers who attacked the gold-laden Spanish ships on their return trip to Spain. Just as in Europe, the countries continued warring with one another. Civilization had come to the New World.

To this day, historians argue the merits of Columbus and his actions. Was he really trying to usher in a new era in which "unwashed heathens" could be cleansed in baptism? Or was his "discovery" merely the first assault in the rape of a continent? Perhaps the truth lies somewhere in between, a mixture of good and bad resulting from the inevitable forging of cultures that would have collided even if Columbus never existed.

Columbus wasn't the first European to reach America. The Vikings landed in North America centuries before. And there is some evidence that a group of Irish monks also made the journey long before Columbus. In fact, some writers have suggested that Columbus was merely following maps made by Portuguese explorers who'd recently made the trip across the Atlantic in secret. According to this argument, Columbus surreptitiously came into possession of the very maps used by the Portuguese navigators and that was why Isabella and Ferdinand suddenly changed their minds and backed Columbus after they'd previously dismissed his ideas as ludicrous.

Another map often claimed to be in Columbus's possession is the mysterious "Vinland Map." This map was said to have been of Viking origin and allegedly was produced fifty years before Columbus sailed to America. Supposedly a medieval map of the known world, it shows North America, or "Vinland," as a huge island in the Atlantic Ocean. Since it first appeared in 1957, scientists have variously proved it to be a hoax and, as more sophisticated dating techniques were used, proved it to be authentic. According to a May 10, 1987, *New York Times* article by Malcolm W. Browne, "Map May Be From Vikings After All," the Vinland Map is still causing great debate among the specialists who are studying it.

No matter what maps Columbus had in his possession, no matter who came before or after him, the fact remains that it was *Columbus's* voyage that permanently altered the course of history by opening up trade between the New and Old World. And though the story of his discovery is well known, the forces that compelled him to make that discovery are often dismissed or downplayed. Such things as messages from God, spectral visitations, and prophecies haunt many historians. Others tend to shrug them off or treat them cavalierly as minor miracles that *may* have happened along the way.

It is through such visions that history can be seen and made.

## The Secret Map

There is one map that beyond all doubt was in Columbus's possession, an unearthly map with mystical directions charting the geography of the soul. More than anything else, it led him to the shores of the New World.

It was a map that many mystics before and after him have followed, equally convinced that it had been created specifically to chart *their* destiny and thus the destiny of the world. The map was the Bible, specifically the Book of Isaiah, which Columbus repeatedly quoted and interpreted as referring directly to him and his actions.

It's interesting to note that some of Columbus's real-life events mirrored things he first encountered in the Book of Isaiah. Toward the end of the first crossing, Columbus was standing on the deck of the *Santa María* when a strange light appeared in the sky. The brilliantly glowing light split the dark night ahead. Like a star over Bethlehem, it was guiding the way.

Columbus saw it as definite proof that they were on the right course and that land would soon be sighted.

But the elusive light remained unseen by the other men aboard the ship. Perhaps they were tired of seeing visions. After all, they'd all shared a previous hallucination when some of the men sighted land at night, seeing tall cliffs standing before them. Soon word spread to other men, and they all saw the cliffs clearly before them.

But the cliffs stood on a foundation of clouds. In the morning, there was no land to be found. (Interestingly enough, the day after Columbus spotted the light singular in the sky, taking it as a sign that land was near, the rest of the crew spotted land. This time it was real.)

Perhaps the light that shone for Christopher Columbus was the same inner light that had illuminated his soul for decades now. Or perhaps it was a spark from the pages of the Book of Isaiah, the biblical chart Columbus often claimed referred to him and his actions. For the Book of Isaiah contains this passage: "The people who walked in darkness have seen a great light. Upon those who dwelt in the land of gloom a light has shone."

Another passage from the Book of Isaiah dovetails nicely with how Columbus repeatedly brought back natives from the West Indies to the court of Spain: "Bring back my sons from afar and my daughters from the ends of the earth; everyone who is named as mine whom I created for my glory, whom I formed and made."

Justification for the wholesale looting of the New World can be found in the passage ". . . For the riches of the sea shall be emptied out before you, the wealth of nations shall be brought to you." Since many explorers, as well as the monarchs who supported them, firmly believed God took an active interest in their every thought and deed, it is possible to see how a passage such as this one could be interpreted as condoning just about anything that brought money into the royal coffers: "All the vessels of the sea are assembled with the ships of Tharsis in the lead, to bring your children from afar with their silver and gold, in the name of the Lord, your God, the Holy One of Israel, who has glorified you."

Columbus also had a voice that guided him, a voice that

spoke to him while he was in a trance. The voice, of course, was God himself, speaking to his Admiral of the Ocean Seas. Columbus wrote of this phenomenon himself, comparing the voice to a quiet but riveting sound that put him into a trancelike stage. He also had visions of himself in the heavens, arms outstretched, leading the faithful of the world into paradise.

For Columbus was also an Admiral of the Spiritual Seas. He wrote extensively about his metaphysical voyages in letters, memoirs, and his *Book of Prophecies*, which are widely available in translations to this day. One source that combines a look at Columbus's own writings with an incisive view of the Admiral himself is the beautifully written 1940 book by Spanish diplomat Salvador de Madariaga, *Christopher Columbus, Being the Life of the Very Magnificent Lord Don Cristobal Colon*.

Included in Madariaga's book is a long letter Columbus wrote to the king and queen about a violent encounter on one of his later explorations when his ships were stranded by bad weather and his thoughts were devoted to surviving a group of vengeance-minded Indian warriors. The Admiral was overcome with despair, fearing the death tolls would mount and his latest expedition would come to ruin.

And then he heard a voice he could not disavow. God had heard his plea for help. According to Columbus's letter, God spoke of the help he'd given Columbus in the past and the help he'd give to him in the future: ''Of the shackles of the Ocean Sea, which were bound with such strong chains, He gave thee the keys; and thou wast obeyed in so many lands and didst win such honored renown among Christians! What more did He do for the people of Israel when He led them out of Egypt?''

The letter continues to quote God in incredible detail about the promises to Columbus that would be kept and that the Admiral had nothing to fear. The tribulations would pass.

There were other moments in Columbus's life when God took a direct hand in his fate, appearing in visions in times of trouble or doubt or coming to him as a voice that placed him in a trance when he needed direction.

One peculiar incident involves three wise men who proved to be as elusive as they were illusive. On Columbus's second journey to the New World, when his men were exploring Cuba, they sighted tall, light-skinned men in white robes walking with the Indians. But these mysterious priestlike beings were never seen again, though Columbus made a lot of effort to track them down. Either they were as mysterious as Columbus believed, or they were smart native priests who knew what happened to other natives who welcomed Columbus and were spirited off to Europe like a prize catch.

On this second trip to the Indies in September of 1493, Columbus came with a large force of ships, soldiers, and colonists. It was a good thing, too.

They'd run out of colonists. The first group of men he'd left behind on Fort Navidad on the island of Haiti had so abused the peaceful natives that the natives revolted, burned the fort to the ground, killed the soldiers, and took back the native wives the colonists had helped themselves to. Perhaps the colonists had prematurely decided they'd discovered the Garden of Eden with all of its attendant pleasures; according to most accounts, the men had several wives each and were living like kings.

In fact, Columbus wouldn't discover the Garden of Eden until his third voyage, when he traveled along the majestic Orinoco River in Venezuela. One of the prevailing myths at the time was that the Garden of Eden was a very real place on earth.

Since Columbus *knew* that somewhere on earth was the Garden of Eden, in his mind it was only logical that God would guide him to it. There was only one flaw in this idea as he sailed along the Orinoco River. If this indeed was the Garden of Eden, what about the Indians that were living in it? Wouldn't they be God's chosen ones, rather than unenlightened heathens? And wouldn't that mean that the warlike colonists were invading heaven on earth?

Such questions were insignificant beside the greater enterprise God had tasked Columbus with—bringing back enough gold to fund another Crusade to the Holy Land. This idea helped create another myth later on when undreamt-of armadas of gold-laden ships made their way back to Spain. Many people made the connection that this New World had to be the legendary site of King Solomon's mines.

To Columbus this largess was proof that by faithfully following the word of God, as it was written or spoken in his ear, he was advancing God's glorious plan.

With such divine counsel guiding him, it's little wonder that Columbus himself would ultimately turn to prophecy himself when he saw the world around him going in the wrong direction—turning away from the taking of Jerusalem.

But despite his mystical bent, in many ways Columbus was a practical man. In fact, if not for the seaman's skills he acquired in his early years along with his ambition and innate sense of command, he might never have reached a position in society where the kings and queens of Europe would take him seriously.

## The Rise and Fall of Christopher Columbus

There were other influences at work upon the mysterious Genoese who obscured his past in order to secure his future. For Columbus did not spring forth into Ferdinand and Isabella's court an immaculately conceived sea captain. There were years of plying his trade at sea, up and down the African coast—a trade that may have included a profitable stint as a corsair or privateer, as suggested by Salvador de Madariaga. One of the questions Madariaga raises in his book is how Columbus managed to amass substantial wealth after just a short time at sea. (Shortly after he turned twenty, Columbus returned from his voyages with enough money to pay off his father's substantial debts, perhaps more than could be expected from the wages of a young hand on a merchant ship.)

Though Columbus hid much of his past from those he sought to sponsor his expeditions, it is known that at one time he was in the service of the mystical-minded René of

Anjou, a Renaissance king who held lands throughout Europe. According to *Heraldry of the Royal Families of Europe* by Jiri Louda and Michael Maclagan, René claimed kingship over Naples, Hungary, and Jerusalem, although his greatest strengths were in Provence and Lorraine. Good King René, as he is often known, had only an illusory reign over Jerusalem, since the European Crusaders had long been chased out of the Middle East. One of René's many goals was to reclaim the throne of Jerusalem for Christianity. In this light, we can see Columbus as one of René's knights off on a remarkable quest for Jerusalem who ultimately would find himself floating in a wooden grail called the *Santa María*.

Columbus detailed some of his early experiences in a letter to Spain's monarchs: "It happened to me that King Reynel . . . sent me to Tunis to seize the galleas *Fernandina*." While working for King René, or Reynel, Columbus was in charge of the raid to take possession of the ship, a swashbuckling captain who ruled his with a calculating hand. As Columbus explained in the letter, his men weren't eager to take the vessel, thinking they didn't have enough men or ships to guarantee success. When they pressed Columbus to return to Marseille for more fighting men and ships, Columbus falsely told them that was the course he had set. In fact, they were still sailing toward Tunis.

This kind of deception was repeated later on in his first voyage to America when his men grew worried about the great distance they were from home as they sailed into the unknown. In one of his more down-to-earth moods, Columbus simply kept two logs. In his private log he recorded the actual distance the ships had traveled. In the log he showed to his men, he recorded a much smaller distance so they wouldn't think they'd traveled past the point of no return.

This willingness to deceive remained with Columbus throughout his career. On one of his later journeys when his crew sailed around Cuba and found it to be an island, he forced them to swear that it wasn't an island. He wanted it to be considered as part of the Asian mainland and thus prove that he'd succeeded in sailing west to Asia. A man who could connect an island to the mainland by sheer force of will was no one to trifle with.

Even so, it took considerable effort for him to evolve from a successful merchant or corsair to an Admiral of the Ocean Sea.

His star began to rise when he married Felipe Perestrello e Moniz, the daughter of a prominent Portuguese sea captain and knight of Christ. From then on, Columbus began to cultivate friendships among respected mariners, clergymen, and advisers to the royal courts of Europe. These friendships ultimately paid off when King Ferdinand and Queen Isabella finally bestowed three ships, ninety men, and the title of Admiral of the Ocean Seas upon the man they considered a fanatic who just might be onto something.

Crucial to Columbus's quest was the support of Franciscan monks who were also well-versed in geography and cosmology. They provided him with maps and letters of introduction to the court of Isabella and Ferdinand and vouched for the credibility of his plan to sail west to Asia.

One of Columbus's chief backers from the clergy was Friar Perez, who had considerable influence on Isabella because he had previously served as her royal confessor. It was chiefly through his efforts that Columbus finally won approval for his voyages.

The Franciscans stood beside Columbus in the beginning—and they stood by him in the end when he returned from his fourth voyage a bitter man whose services were no longer sought. It was clear that he would not lead the holy armies to Jerusalem. It was also clear that his expected share of the wealth flooding back to Spain would not come his way. And that was perhaps his greatest misfortune.

It wasn't greed that made him want the gold. He wanted it for the glory of God. Right up to the end, he believed that God had guided him to find the New World and bring back gold along with the great harvest of souls. This would provide not only the necessary Crusaders, but enough gold to bankroll such a huge undertaking. But the monarchs had other things in mind than furthering the messianic cause of Christopher Columbus.

## The Visionary Columbus

Columbus had followed prophecies all his life. Now, in his waning years, he made prophecies.

His aptly titled work, *The Book of Prophecies*, combines the biblical prophecies he claimed he fulfilled with some of his own apocalyptic views. According to Columbus, it was clear to anyone who took the time to read the prophecies that God meant for him to lead the last Crusade to the Holy Land.

Now that Columbus had discovered the uncharted lands whose inhabitants would be converted to Christianity and begin the final march to restore God's kingdom on earth, the countdown to Apocalypse and the Second Coming had begun. Following the tenets of many prophets and clergymen who believed the world had only a seven-thousand-year run, Columbus decided that 6845 years had already gone by and, since he'd fulfilled some of the conditions for the Second Coming, there were only 155 years left on the earthly timetable.

The need to retake the Holy Land was still crucial in Columbus's mind. But it finally became clear to the Admiral that the same goal was not shared by Isabella and Ferdinand.

And so in the end the aging Columbus turned to an unearthly monarch, aware that perhaps soon he would once again enter a new world.

# 9
# Incan Armageddon

## *I Return of the Gods?*

In the year 1530 the Incan civilization in South America had a highly advanced culture that saw to the needs of a population of nearly 16 million people spread out over nearly three thousand miles of territory.

In the year 1533, that same civilization was in ruins. The king of the Incas had been strangled to death. Tens of thousands of his people had been murdered. The wealth of a nation had been robbed.

This great catastrophe occurred simply because the Incas welcomed "divine messengers" to their shores. At least in the beginning, they thought the fierce-looking white-skinned newcomers were godly messengers. Many of the Incas believed this was one of their well-known prophecies coming true.

According to the prophecy the bearded white god known

as Viracocha, or the Creator God, would return to their country during the reign of the current Inca ruler, leading an unknown race of men.

One of the chief supporters of this prophecy happened to be the ruler of the empire. That is the reason why the Spanish adventurer Francisco Pizarro and his force of under two hundred men and horses were allowed to come into the interior of the country after they landed on the shore of Peru.

## The Message Is Death

Atahualpa, the new king, or Inca, of the region, believed the strangely garbed men with their wondrous animals and regal bearing were the honor guard of the new incarnation of Viracocha—Francisco Pizarro. Many of the Incas who'd seen the conquistadors believed that man and horse were one creature and that the armor they wore was a magical skin.

As Incan couriers spread the news from town to town, the newcomers were portrayed in a more miraculous light with each successive telling. The Inca sent envoys to arrange a meeting with the celestial messengers at a town called Cajamarca.

Pizarro agreed. Then he and his celestial messengers began pillaging the countryside on their way to Cajamarca.

On the appointed day, Atahualpa waited in the town square with thousands of his people to greet the messengers of Viracocha. But instead of coming out into the open to meet the king, Pizarro's conquistadors remained out of sight and prepared an ambush for the Incan ruler.

A priest traveling with Pizarro came forward and offered a Bible to Atahualpa. Since the Incan culture was based on rituals, symbols, and word of mouth, the printed pages were meaningless to Atahualpa. He discarded the Bible.

Interpreting this as a slight to their highly developed spiritual sensibilities, the conquistadors opened up with their muskets, then charged out with horse and sword and slaughtered thousands of the Incan people who'd come to welcome them.

There were no deaths among the Spaniards.

Atahualpa was captured alive.

## A King's Ransom and a Baptism in Blood

Threatened with horrible death by Pizarro, the Incan ruler offered to pay a kingly ransom in exchange for his life by filling two rooms with gold and silver.

Pizarro agreed to the bargain.

Tons of gold and silver relics and ceremonial objects were brought in from all over the empire, which Pizarro quickly melted down.

As soon as the Inca had fulfilled his part of the bargain, Pizarro ordered him killed. But the Inca was shown one more kindness by the divine messengers from across the sea. If Atahualpa agreed to become a Christian, then his captors wouldn't burn him at the stake. Instead, these kindly messengers would strangle him to death. The king of one of the largest empires in the world agreed to the terms.

And so the priest baptized him.

And the soldiers strangled him.

The Inca's death was an omen of things to come. More and more conquistadors arrived, marching inland to slaughter, enslave, mutilate, torture, murder, and terrorize the Incan people in their endless search for gold and converts to their faith.

Several Incan armies eventually rebelled against Spanish rule, but they, too, were destroyed. Just as the prophecy had said, an unknown race had come from across the sea to subdue their empire.

But the conquistadors didn't always live that long to enjoy their spoils. Pizarro himself was killed by a fellow conquistador in a feud over the spoils. Several other members of Pizarro's party met fitting violent deaths—seeding the land they'd come to conquer with their own blood.

## II Aztec Assassination

The wholesale slaughter of the Incan people was an eerie echo of the fate that fell upon the Aztec Empire, which ruled much of what is today Mexico.

Like the Incan ruler, the leader of the Aztecs, Montezuma, was a firm believer in prophecies and magic. Montezuma also believed the gods had a direct hand in the everyday life of his people. For that reason he ordered huge numbers of sacrifices to appease them, on occasion having thousands of people killed at one time.

·This practice directly contradicted the wishes of a creator god named Quetzalcoatl, who, according to Aztec belief, had been driven from Mexico by demonic entities.

Among the Aztec prophecies was one that told of Quetzalcoatl's return—when he would destroy whoever broke his commandments.

A shape-changing god who appeared in a winged serpentine form as well as a man with light skin and a dark beard, Quetzalcoatl's impending return coincided with the arrival in the year 1519 of Hernando Cortés—commander of a five-hundred-man expedition from Cuba.

With Montezuma's supernatural fear of Quetzalcoatl holding him back from fighting the troops of Cortés, the conquistadors were able to push themselves into the capital city at Tenochtitlán, where they demanded tribute.

Montezuma responded with tremendous amounts of treasure.

The demands kept up. Cortés wanted more and more treasure. Finally, after observing Cortés' blasphemous behavior in an Aztec temple, Montezuma realized that this could not be the god he'd imagined him to be. But it was too late for Montezuma to correct his mistakes. The white gods had already struck at the heart of his empire.

The Aztec warriors and advisers who'd been warning Montezuma all along about the conquistadors finally revolted, stoning Montezuma and taking up arms against Cortés' army, which fought its way out of the city with all the gold it could carry.

Pursued by the Aztec warriors in a battle that lasted several days, the conquistadors managed to kill the war chief of the Aztecs in a last-ditch counterattack.

The leaderless Aztecs withdrew.

So did Cortés.

He returned a half-year later with a huge army with a core of nearly one thousand professional soldiers and an auxiliary army of Indians who'd harbored enmity for the Aztecs and saw their chance for revenge by allying themselves with Cortés.

Cortés' army besieged the town for months before leading an attack on the Aztecs that resulted in nearly fifty thousand casualties and total defeat of the Aztecs.

The white man had come.

And the gods had gone.

# 10

## The Men in the Iron Mask

### The Sun King and His Satanic Queen

Two of the greatest mysteries surrounding the reign of Louis XIV, the Sun King, have come down to us as the Affair of the Chambre Ardente and the Man in the Iron Mask. And both of those famous cases just may be connected through the person of Madame de Montespan, a courtesan who bore several children for the king.

In her efforts to remain as his illicit queen, Madame de Montespan brought about the wrack and ruin of hundreds of people who were hanged, tortured under interrogation, imprisoned, exiled, or burned at the stake.

Once a woman of incomparable beauty and charm who was the reigning queen of courtesans, when Madame de Montespan eventually began to lose her figure she also began to lose her control over the Sun King. Fearing that she could no longer compete against the many potential replacements for her position as the royal mistress, Madame de Montespan initiated a plan to poison the king himself.

The plan involved a poisoned letter treated with a chemical that would eventually kill Louis the XIV after he touched it. But the plot failed when the poisoner who was supposed to deliver the letter was unable to reach the king.

Soon after this episode, King Louis XIV learned of Madame de Montespan's involvement not only in the poisoning ring but also in an underground church that specialized in black magic and murder. This subterranean world of satanic intrigues was populated by some of the most noble—and decadent—names in France.

Since many of King Louis's aristocratic friends also happened to be the targets of this satanic ring, he moved quickly to set up a special investigating committee to uncover and then stamp out the criminal network of poisoners and blasphemers.

This investigation was headed by Nicholas de Reynie, the police commissioner of Paris, who began an exhaustive and intensive investigation in the French underworld. It happened to be an investigation that took him to the heights of French society.

But King Louis XIV was determined to get to the heart of the matter, and he supported his police commissioner no matter where the trail lay. Although not all of the guilty parties implicated in the affair would be punished, at least all of their stories would be collected and considered. The king wanted to find out all of the facts, no matter how embarrassing to him or any members of the court.

With the backing of the king and his own brutally effective methods of interrogation, La Reynie continued the investigation and soon uncovered the secret history of black magic and murder that for several years had been contaminating the cream of French society.

Witnesses presented their testimony before a court that came to be known as the Chambre Ardente (the Burning Chamber), which aggressively prosecuted a select number of those involved.

The Chamber just as aggressively tried to cover up the activities of others who were involved, mainly influential members of royalty and none other than the woman who was responsible for much of the misery and murder—Madame de Montespan.

## Poisoned Minds

Shimmering candlelight glittered on the dark walls of the hidden room in one of the finest houses in all of Paris—the palatially furnished residence of Catherine Deshayes, who was known as Madame La Voisin.

In their black robes and masks the small group of aristocrats stood silently, hypnotized by the false majesty of the bloody and blasphemous ritual taking place before them. Not satisfied with their lofty position of power and prestige at the court of King Louis XIV, they had turned to black magic to achieve their aims, following the lead of a debased priest and swindler named Abbé Guibourg who concocted the ceremonies as well as many of the infamous potions handed out by La Voisin.

Now, lying upon the altar, wax burning on her bare stomach, was Madame de Montespan, mistress of King Louis XIV. Her amorous attentions and intrigues were no longer enough to keep Louis's attention concentrated on her. So she had turned to love potions—and poisons—to magically maintain her hold over the Sun King as well as eliminate her enemies and competitors. The voluptuous mistress had become a regular member of the underground church taking root in the Parisian underworld.

In Charles Mackay's famous 1841 chronicle of the absurd impetus behind many of history's greatest movements, *Extraordinary Delusions and the Madness of Crowds*, he discussed the foundation of the scandal that would soon rock all of France and expose the activities of highborn royalty as lowlife criminals. This scandal involved hundreds of swindlers, as well as the swindled.

It also exposed Madame de Montespan as one of the main players in the devil's game.

Many of the players would end up on the gallows, and just as many—particularly the titled ones—went on with their lives with just one more covert crime only mentioned in whispers.

The cycle of poison and paranoia began when a beautiful woman by the name of Madame de Brinvilliers came under the spell of a man released from the Bastille. Known as Saint Croix, he specialized in manufacturing poison in liquid form as well as a slower-acting poison called "succession powder," so named because it was used in many intrigues.

After testing the drug to determine its potency, Madame de Brinvilliers gave it to her father. The poison killed him within ten days. She also invited her brothers to Paris, and when they fell victim to the poison, she became not only a beautiful woman, but a beautiful heiress and murderer.

Saint Croix and his disciple de Brinvilliers fell out soon afterward over distribution of her inheritance and her desire to kill the aging, decadent husband she was separated from.

Though the husband survived, Saint Croix died soon after from inhaling the fumes of the chemicals used to make his poisons. As a result of Saint Croix falling victim to his own poisons, many of his papers and his detailed records of his finances came into the possession of the authorities, who now had evidence of Madame de Brinvilliers' guilt.

Learning that she'd been found out, Madame de Brinvilliers escaped to England one step ahead of the law. She returned years later in disguise, seeking refuge in a convent.

Although she had apparently escaped the authorities for several years, the law of Karma was still working against her. Soon after she entered the convent she was courted by a police officer named Desgrais, who disguised himself as a priest with amorous intent. Madame de Brinvilliers left the convent for a rendezvous with her illicit admirer— who immediately arrested her and brought her into custody.

## The Inheritors of Evil

Though de Brinvilliers was caught, the techniques perfected by her and Saint Croix quickly spread through the underworld of Paris, chiefly by Catherine Deshayes (who became known as La Voisin) and a fortune-teller named La Dame Vigoreux. They embellished Saint Croix's techniques by acting as midwives and fortune-tellers to assemble intelligence on their would-be targets to convince them of their spiritual abilities or to gather information for blackmail.

Their modern-day counterparts are those fortune-tellers to the stars who have evolved their techniques as well as their titles (seers, channelers, psychic counselors) to reap great profits for being able to read the wants and needs of their subjects and package them in paranormal patois.

But La Voisin added something extra to the mix—an acute knowledge of chemistry, which allowed her to give her clients something to help along any of the curses she offered. She often helped her clients improve their love lives and their fortunes by providing poison to do away with their aging husbands.

In *Look for the Woman*, Jay Robert Nash cites the first casualty of La Voisin as a Judge Leféron, whose wife sought out poison as a final cure.

With seers like La Voisin and La Dame Vigoreux at work, the fortunes of their clients were often easy to predict—tragedy was in the air.

After a long investigation, both La Voisin and La Dame Vigoreux were brought to justice.

But the most crucial information came from La Voisin. She was the most notorious and the most well-connected poisoner in the underworld ring. Nicholas de la Reynie obtained detailed statements from Madame La Voisin, members of her family, and the corrupt associates who helped her carry out her black masses.

This questioning provided leads to many other charlatans and murderers fleecing the French aristocracy by selling them charms for eternal love, curses for their enemies, performing necromantic rites for them, and holding black masses.

This was one of those few cases where black masses and murders actually were being conducted. Rather than the usual phony charges leveled against innocent victims or rivals, the charges against La Voisin and her retinue were authentic.

Infants *were* murdered for rites in the addled black mass. Potions *were* handed out—absurd love potions as well as poison. Though several other poisoners and fortune-tellers were involved in the same sort of crimes, the focus of the Chambre Ardente remained on Madame La Voisin.

She had been responsible for hundreds of murders of infants and countless cases of poisoning. She and her defrocked priest, Abbé Guibourg, had made an industry of murder and black magic, ultimately leading to a plot by Madame de Montespan to win back the affections of King Louis XIV.

This attempt at regicide no doubt sealed her fate.

As Charles Mackay wrote about the execution of La Voisin and La Dame Vigoreux in *Popular Delusions*,

''They were both tried, found guilty, and burned alive in the Place de Gréve, on the 22nd of February, 1680, after their heads had been bored through with a red-hot iron, and then cut off.''

The cruel treatment was allegedly in payment for the hundreds of murders they'd committed by poison and by sacrificing infants at their black masses.

But La Voisin and La Dame Vigoreux were not the only ones who received severe sentences. About fifty more people involved in the black-magic marketing of poisons and spells were hanged. Several others were imprisoned or banished from France. In many cases, if the guilty parties were noble or influential enough, the records of their involvement simply vanished—almost as if by magic.

## The List of La Voisin

The list of La Voisin's clients that was delivered into the hands of the commission included such well-known names as the Marshal de Luxembourg, the Countess de Soisons, and the Duchess de Bouillon. Another reputed customer was the celebrated poet and playwright Racine. But because of their position and reputation, they avoided punishment and often were let off without a reprimand.

An often-repeated incident recounted in Mackay's *Popular Delusions* involves an encounter between the Duchess de Bouillon after she was arrested and questioned by La Reynie, president of the chamber. When he asked her if it was ever possible to really see the devil as many of the members of the black magic circle had claimed, she gave him a wicked reply: "Oh yes, I see him now. He is in the form of a little ugly old man, exceedingly ill-natured, and is dressed in the robes of a Counseller of State."

The counselor learned nothing more from her—since she was soon freed because of her influential friends at the court of King Louis. But the Chambre Ardente amassed a great amount of information on other participants in the black masses and poison intrigues, much of it sealed away until the Bastille was stormed and many of the sensitive documents came to light.

And, of course, many of the members of King Louis's circle also knew the names of the participants. As a result, word leaked out in letters and memoirs.

One of the people allegedly involved in the various intrigues of the time—particularly with Madame de Montespan—was a man who may have achieved immortality by the pen of Alexandre Dumas in the classic tale that is today widely known as "The Man in the Iron Mask."

## Who Was That Masked Man?

The other great mystery from the reign of King Louis XIV is the identity of the noble prisoner who was kept masked and incommunicado while he was imprisoned by the king.

Though he was moved from prison to prison, the Man

in the Iron Mask was always kept isolated from other prisoners. However, he was given special treatment and at times was even allowed to have a personal valet.

But the prisoner wasn't allowed to speak to anyone under penalty of death—for himself as well as the person who heard what he had to say.

What great secret could he hold to require such care? And why were his features masked? Either the prisoner was of such a noble birth that King Louis couldn't bear to have him killed—or else he'd committed such a heinous crime that his punishment was to be kept alive but cut off from human contact for the rest of his life.

Another theory involves not just his identity, but his heritage. According to this theory, the Man in the Iron Mask is a brother of the Sun King, or perhaps a half brother. But apparently he was also involved in a number of intrigues that convinced King Louis he had to be kept under lock and key—and *mask*.

The birth of King Louis XIV had often been considered a miracle, since his father had proved incapable of having a child. According to many, this was as much a matter of impotence as inclination.

With the need to produce an heir for King Louis XIII— at least according to this hypothesis—a surrogate father was brought in to impregnate Queen Anne. This substitution was arranged by influential members close to the throne—perhaps the cardinals who wielded so much power in the affairs of state.

The surrogate sire was successful, and King Louis XIV

was born. But apparently the Sun King had a brother or a half brother by this same father. Since the familial resemblance was similar enough to raise questions in the eyes of the public, this half brother was spirited away and kept in the half-darkness of the mask.

Questions remain about the motive behind the man's imprisonment as well as the mask itself. Some writers have said it was a cloth mask. Others claim it actually was made of metal. One thing most writers are in agreement upon is that the mask, whatever it was made of, had a section, possibly spring-hinged, that could be raised so the prisoner could take his meals.

A familiar name surfaces in any of the investigations into the identity of the Man in the Iron Mask: Madame de Montespan.

As mentioned earlier, she was constantly searching for some potion or power that would keep Louis XIV in her thrall. Since much of her efforts in this regard depended upon black magic, it's interesting to see who some of her companions were.

The particular rituals that she took part in were blasphemous parodies of the Catholic mass in which her body was the altar. And in order to consummate this wretched ceremony, a male partner was necessary.

Many times the partner was alleged to be the defrocked priest who held the service. But other men were involved. And one of these men who allegedly served as Madame de Montespan's unholy partner was Eustache Dauger, who came from a military family that was very close to the throne of France. Eustache had a very mysterious background that involved him in various intrigues that often resulted in spells of imprisonment. But he always seemed to avoid punishment for his ways because of his connections.

In fact, Eustache's father was a commander of the musketeers and on occasion served as one of King Louis XIII's royal bodyguards. And perhaps he served Queen Anne in a much more intimate manner by fathering Louis XIV.

This would make Eustache Dauger a half brother to King Louis, possibly a roguish half brother who may have used his resemblance to the king in subtle forms of blackmail to keep himself out of jail. Or perhaps he made demands that eventually pushed the king past his limits.

But if Eustache Dauger was indeed the Man in the Iron Mask, he may have been imprisoned in this highly unusual manner as a form of lenient but permanent punishment for having the ability to double as Madame de Montespan's lover in the black magic ceremonies.

## The Mad Musketeer

Eustache Dauger was not just someone from the street without a connection to the court of Louis XIV. Like his brothers, Dauger had seen considerable experience in the service of the Sun King, whose wars of expansion required and rewarded soldiers who served him well.

But Dauger had also earned a reputation as an impulsive man who was constantly involved in duels and brawls and intrigues. As a young man he'd spent some time in prison, until his benefactors used their influence at the court to earn his release.

Dauger, like D'Artagnan and the other raucous musketeers Alexandre Dumas would later write about in some of the nearly three hundred novels credited to his name, was never one to stay out of trouble. Perhaps he felt a man of his position could always evade punishment—or perhaps he felt that some of the throne-rattling secrets he possessed would keep him out of harm's way.

Though he was a brawler and a roguish sort, Dauger didn't meet his match until he encountered Madame de Montespan, who, as mentioned earlier, had a murderous involvement with black magic and a ring of poisoners. Because of his character and his position, many earlier writers have suggested that Dauger was in fact the man who accompanied Madame de Montespan to La Voisin's Parisian mansion for her "trysts with the devil."

To a soldier such as Dauger, it probably appeared as one more affectation of the addled rich. One more mad eccentricity on the part of the voluptuous courtesan. But unfortunately some of these rites later on involved murder of newborns—by defrocked priests.

Whether or not Dauger was de Montespan's lover, he was imprisoned for crimes related to the ring of poisoners and black magicians plying their trade to highborn clients all across France. Despite the fact that he was held on criminal charges, Dauger was given exceptional treatment. Apprehended on personal orders of the king, Dauger was escorted to prison under the guard of a warden named

Saint-Mars, who would in effect become the Man in the Iron Mask's personal warden until the day the prisoner died.

At this point—March of 1669—Dauger vanishes from history.

And the Man in the Iron Mask makes his debut.

The closeness in time of Dauger's arrest and the circumstances connecting him to the royal household makes him one of the most likely—if unlucky—claimants to the title of Man in the Iron Mask, the man who spent the rest of his life caged off from his fellow man.

## The Men in the Mask

While Dauger seems the most likely candidate for the role of the Man in the Iron Mask, there have been persuasive arguments for a number of other unusual figures caught in the web of intrigue surrounding the Sun King.

In his thorough study of the reign of Louis XIV, Voltaire argued that the Man in the Mask was none other than a brother of Louis XIV. According to Voltaire, this brother was the rightful heir to the throne who was imprisoned by King Louis but kept alive because the impostor king couldn't bring himself to kill someone of his own blood. This theory advances the idea that the brother was allegedly fathered by Cardinal Mazarin, since King Louis XIII was believed incapable of creating a heir.

But this also raises another question: Who fathered the son who went on to become King Louis the XIV? Was this second child the actual child of Louis XIII, or was it another surrogate father like Mazarin?

Another serious candidate for the unenviable position of Man in the Iron Mask was an aide to the Duke of Mantua named Ercole Mattioli, who played a part in secret negotiations between the Duke and Louis XIV concerning Louis's taking control of a province called Casale.

Since the negotiations were undermining treaties the duke had with other parties in the area, there was considerable fallout when Mattioli leaked some of the details to Louis's enemies.

Louis had Mattioli taken prisoner in Italy and quickly locked away from sight of any of his friends. Perhaps the mask was used to prevent any of Mattioli's patrons from knowing where he was kept, or even that he was now a royal prisoner.

According to this theory, Mattioli then began a series of stays in a number of prisons before he was taken to the Bastille.

Bolstering the theory that Mattioli was the Man in the Mask was the statement by a king's warden named Jonca that Mattioli was listed on prison rolls as M. Marchiel. Later on, when the Man in the Iron Mask was buried, his name was listed as Marchiolly.

Some of the royal secrets were revealed years later when the Bastille itself became prisoner of the French people during the revolution. In the backlash against royalty, the remaining archives from the period of King Louis XIV were given to the public by a Charpentier, who exposed yet another plausible claimant to the Man in the Iron Mask.

According to the documents he found, Charpentier said that it was widely believed by members of Louis's court that the Man in the Mask was the bastard son of Queen Anne before she gave birth to Louis. The father in this case supposedly was the Duke of Buckingham. The reason this man was kept in the mask was his alleged resemblance to Louis XIV—based on this likeness, he could have laid a claim to the throne.

There may be even more candidates for the royal prisoner of King Louis XIV, but whoever it was—and whatever the reason he was secreted away—will no doubt be masked from history.

# 11

## The Divine Rites of Kings

### The Caribbean King

The Caribbean island of Jamaica is one of the most beautiful places on earth, with a warm climate and a warm and friendly people who have a gently mystical outlook on life.

It is also an island haunted by its past of slavery. In the 1600s and 1700s, both Spanish and English plantation owners made it a slave center for the West Indies. The original Arawak Indians had died long before as a result of the enforced labor the "civilizing" powers exacted on the natives.

When the Spanish lost their control of the island to the British, it became a haven for The Brethren, a homicidal fraternity of pirates and privateers, including the notorious Henry Morgan, who sacked Spanish capitals in Panama and Venezuela before being rewarded with the governorship of Jamaica.

Though the pirates eventually were brought under control, misery remained a constant due to the ever-increasing number of slaves who were imported from Africa to work on the sugarcane plantations.

Crammed onto overcrowded ships where they were often exposed to disease and starvation, many of the slaves died on the trip across the Atlantic. A good number of those who survived found themselves facing even more horrible conditions when they were left at the mercy of the cruel overlords on the plantations.

To the eyes of the slavers, the supply of labor was unlimited. They took advantage of the tribal warfare in Africa, which resulted in a large number of captives who were then sold to the slavers for delivery to the plantations in the West Indies.

Soon the number of slaves was far out of proportion to the colonists, with a ratio of more than twenty slaves to every colonist in the mid-1700s. Furthermore, in many cases the African slaves had come from a higher cultural position than the plantation owners who now believed they owned them body and soul. Many of the slaves were actually veteran warriors, and a good number of them were kings and queens in their homeland.

One such member of African royalty was Prince Mansong of Kaarta, a West African kingdom at war with Saharan Moors. The Moors arranged a peace treaty only to entrap Mansong, the premier warrior of Kaarta. And like so many other captives, he was sold into slavery and sent to Jamaica.

Soon after he arrived in Jamaica, he gained a nickname that has lasted to the present day—Three-Fingered Jack.

Mansong worked on a plantation in the Blue Mountains of Jamaica near Kingston. After tiring of the brutal treatment he received for his rebellious spirit, Mansong turned inward, keeping his hatred of the white overlords in check until he eventually was rewarded with some of the freedoms given to trusted slaves.

He used this new ration of freedom to seek out like-minded slaves who were willing to go to war in order to win their real freedom. Gradually, with the help of an African shaman, or Obeah-man, he enlisted a small army of slaves and led them in an uprising against the white colonists.

But Mansong's raid on a white township was thwarted when the local authorities learned of his plans from informants in the slave army and counterattacked with hundreds of troops.

The army was scattered.

Only Mansong kept the fight alive, retreating to the hills to escape the hunting parties.

Then, armed with charms given to him by the Obeah-man who still hid in the hills, he launched a guerrilla war against the colonists and the slaves who had turned against him. Coming down from his mountain hideout, he would suddenly appear in front of his target—almost like a man challenging all comers to a duel, killing or robbing them with frightening regularity.

Because of his fearlessness and his skill as a warrior, Mansong soon gathered a supernatural aura about him— aided by the Obeah charms he wore, which were designed to protect him against all weapons. This alone often caused his ambushed victims to turn and run at the sight of him.

His divine protection, along with pistol and sword, worked for a while. But then on a mountain road he encountered an armed slave who fired back at Mansong, shooting off two of his fingers.

After that unlucky incident, he became known as Three-Fingered Jack and continued his attacks on the male population, black or white.

Since Three-Fingered Jack had been denied his kingdom in Africa, he considered the wild mountain land around him to be his kingdom, and woe to anyone who strayed into it.

His reign lasted a little more than a year—but in that time everyone in the country knew of him and dreaded the name Three-Fingered Jack.

The reward on his head went up from 100 pounds to 200 pounds. With this incentive leading them on, three black men from the region set out to track down Three-Fingered Jack—regardless of the supernatural spell many people believed he'd cast around his hideout. One of the men was the slave who'd previously shot Three-Fingered Jack. The other two were bounty hunters.

The three of them surprised their quarry at his mountain hideout and, after a brief fight, pursued him through the woods. Like an eighteenth-century version of David and Goliath, one of the bounty hunters—a man named Davy—

hurled a rock that struck the giant warrior in the head and killed him instantly.

The king of the mountain was dead.

His head and hand were cut off and carried in a bucket of rum to Kingston so the bounty hunters could lay claim to their reward.

And according to the 1987 *Insight Guide to Jamaica*, there is still a roadside marker in the Blue Mountain foothills in memory of Three-Fingered Jack.

Though Three-Fingered Jack is the more well-known rebel from the time, in 1760 an earlier rebellion was led by another slave who had been a Koromantee chieftain in his African homeland. Named Tacky, his rebellion also was crushed by colonial troops and he was hunted down by Maroons—the descendants of freed Spanish slaves. And like Three-Fingered Jack, he, too, was killed by a man named Davy.

# 12

## The Haunted Highlander

### The Black Watch of Duncan Campbell

Major Duncan Campbell was not the type of man to spook easily. An accomplished soldier, the laird of Inverawe had come to America with the 42nd Highland Regiment at the height of the French and Indian War. The Scottish regiment bolstered an army of British regulars and American colonials, including the legendary founder of the Rangers, Major Robert Rogers. Together they were marching north in an attempt to drive the French troops and their Indian allies from the region.

Campbell's Highland Regiment, known as the Black Watch in the nineteenth century, was nearly one thousand strong and was part of the largest British army yet raised on the Continent. Under the command of General Abercrombie, unaffectionately known by some of his troops as Aunt Abby Cromby, there were approximately fifteen thousand men marching against the French.

Their destination was Fort Carillon, the stronghold of Marquis Louis de Montcalm that was strategically situated on the stretch of land between the upper end of Lake George and the lower end of Lake Champlain. At his greatest strength during the ensuing conflict, Montcalm would have no more than four thousand French troops and Indian allies under his command. Aside from having a smaller army, Montcalm had to defend a position that could be pounded into submission from a number of heights the British artillery could easily reach.

All in all, it looked like the end for Montcalm.

And it looked like another glorious campaign for Duncan Campbell and the Highlanders of the 42nd Regiment.

But there were other forces lurking in the woods.

On their northern trek the British forces passed through the ruins of Fort William Henry, which had been burned to the ground less than a year before, on August 7, 1757. Although the exact number of British and American soldiers and civilians living at the fort at the southern end of Lake George isn't known, estimates place the figure at about two thousand. However many, it wasn't enough. After holding out for six days, wracked by disease and relentless artillery bombardment by Montcalm's troops, Colonel Monro surrendered to General Montcalm. The marquis extended generous terms, promising safe conduct down to the British garrison at Fort Edward near Glens Falls.

But as soon as the prisoners marched out, the massacre began. Abenaki Indians under Montcalm's command rushed into the fort's infirmary and began slaughtering and torturing the wounded. The grisly scalpings, decapitations, and tortures escalated and soon the Indian warriors began pulling prisoners from the long line of captured soldiers and subjecting them to torture and murder.

Hundreds of prisoners were massacred and taken prisoner by the Indians before the French troops intervened, restoring order and escorting the survivors to Fort Edward.

In his 1955 account, *Fort William Henry, A History*, Stanley M. Gifford quotes Major Israel Putnam, a Ranger who came upon the still-smoldering remains of the fort: "Innumerable fragments of human skulls, and bones and carcasses half consumed, were still frying and broiling in the decaying fires . . . More than one hundred women butchered and shockingly mangled, lay upon the ground still weltering in their gore . . ."

Such was life in the wilderness. And death. The Indian war cries and the death screams that filled the air on the day of the massacre nearly a year before still echoed silently and endlessly in the minds of those who passed by.

Though many early accounts claim up to several hundred people were massacred, the more recent scholarship of Professor Ian Steele shows that no more than thirty-five to sixty people were killed. The exaggerated death toll can be attributed to British propaganda about the massacre.

Ironically, Duncan Campbell and the Highland Regiment had earlier been stationed at the site of another massacre. Before marching north against Montcalm, the Highland Regiment was garrisoned in Schenectady along the Mohawk River. There, during a blinding white snowstorm on the night of February 8, 1690, a French and Indian raiding party slipped through the gates of the stockade and methodically began murdering the men, women, and children inside.

These were some of the forces at work in the New World the Highlanders found themselves marching through.

And yet another ghostly force was at work—at least upon the haunted mind of Duncan Campbell.

A Highlander was waiting for him somewhere in the woods. A dead Highlander.

The haunting had begun more than a decade before and an ocean away when a ghostly presence first visited Duncan Campbell in his castle at Inverawe and delivered a fatal warning that now became clearer with every step he took in this green-spired wilderness.

Duncan Campbell was now following an eerie course charted out for him in incredible detail by a spectral cartographer. Despite the overwhelming superiority of the British forces and his considerable experience as a soldier, Duncan Campbell had good reason to believe that he had embarked upon his last march.

## The Visitation

Long before Major Campbell came to America with the Highland Regiment he lived in the Scottish Highlands, the laird of his castle at Inverawe. At the time, the land was alive with blood feuds and skirmishes and brawls, and one such bloody feud literally came to his doorstep.

He was awakened by a man pounding on his castle gate late at night, a wild-eyed man in torn and bloody clothing who was seeking asylum. He claimed he'd been involved in a brawl in which he'd killed a man in a fair fight. And now he was being hunted down by the slain man's friends. He asked for refuge and Duncan Campbell granted it, hiding him in the depths of the castle.

And then he found out who the dead man was.

It was his cousin Donald Campbell. The news was brought to his castle by two armed men who were searching for his kinsman's killer. But the stricken laird sent the searchers away and kept the horrible secret to himself.

After all, he'd given his sacred oath to the fugitive. And Duncan Campbell was the sort of man who would never break his word no matter how tragic the circumstance.

It's no surprise that Duncan Campbell slept uneasily that night. The laird of Inverawe was harboring the man who'd killed his cousin.

And soon he was harboring the cousin himself.

That night Duncan Campbell was suddenly yanked from sleep by a wraithlike man standing beside his bed. A dead man. It was the ghost of Donald Campbell, speaking in a voice that seemed to come from fathomless depths: "Inverawe! Inverawe! Blood has been shed. Shield not the murderer."

In the morning, tormented by the warning of his spectral kinsman, Campbell told the killer he would have to leave. When the fugitive protested that Campbell had given him his word, the laird insisted on a compromise and led him to a secure cave in the mountains. That satisfied Campbell that he was being true to his word and his kinsman at the same time. But it didn't satisfy Donald Campbell.

That night Donald's spirit appeared again, repeating his command not to shield the murderer. When the dawn broke, Campbell went to the cave and found that the man was gone. His cousin's killer had escaped.

The matter was ended. Or so thought Duncan Campbell. But the ghost of his cousin Donald appeared once more. That night he stood beside the laird's bed and delivered an eerie warning: "Farewell, Inverawe! Farewell, till we meet at Ticonderoga!"

The warning meant nothing to Duncan Campbell. He'd never heard of Ticonderoga. But it was such an unusual name, it stayed with him from then on.

From here the story gets stranger.

## Into the Black Forest

The majestic spires of northern New York's Adirondack woods sprawl to the left and right of the Northway that leads from Albany up to the Canadian border. On some stretches of the highway you can still catch glimpses of the past and see the land almost the way the British army must have as it journeyed north. Sheer cliffs rise above the treetops, with silver rivers ribboning down through glacially carved gorges.

But this is just a passing glimpse of the unyielding majesty faced by General Abercrombie's troops two centuries ago. In some places on their march, the trees were so close together that the men could see only a few feet in front of them at any time.

It was in such a shadow-filled wall of trees that a battle began, an unplanned skirmish between advancing British forces and a large French scouting party. In the thick of the woods, where visibility was limited to little more than the man in front or behind, the two forces collided. Then mass confusion and carnage began as deafening musket fire shredded the trees from every corner.

At this point Roger's Rangers, an elite force of guerrilla fighters totally at home in the woods, waded into the French lines and decimated them, killing or capturing more than half of the party before the survivors fled back toward Fort Carillon.

Unfortunately for the British, this promising beginning was the high point of the battle.

Nearer to the fort, the French had created a killing field strewn with barricades of newly cut trees, sharpened stakes, and trenches, making a frontal assault by infantry troops suicidal. This was exactly the tactic chosen by General Abercrombie.

The uneasy sleep of the dead had left its mark on Duncan Campbell on the morning of the battle.

There were two things troubling him as he joined his fellow officers that day. First, he had recently learned that Fort Carillon, as it was called by the French, was known by another name to some of the Indians and American colonials: *Ticonderoga*.

It was the name that had stayed in his mind all these years. A name first uttered by the ghost of his slain kinsman.

Worse, as he told his officers, Duncan Campbell had been visited by the ghost of Donald Campbell one more time. The spirit appeared to him in his tent on the eve of the battle, greeting him with an eerie welcome, saying, "This is Ticonderoga."

And so Duncan Campbell prepared to march into battle, fully convinced that he was cursed to die that day. No matter what his fellow officers said, nothing could change his mind. He felt that his departed cousin Donald Campbell was more conversant with the afterlife and who would soon be on its roster.

Another curse was at work that day. It was the curse of General Abercrombie, who against all common sense had decided not to employ the considerable artillery the British had brought with them. Instead, he decided that the battle would be decided by the courage of his magnificent soldiers.

And so he used *them* as cannon fodder.

The Highlanders and the British regulars were commanded to launch a frontal assault on Fort Ticonderoga. Soon the eerie piping of the Highland Regiment echoed in the woods as they marched forward, scrambling atop the sharpened branches of the *abattis* protecting the earthworks outside the fort, making perfect targets for the French musketmen behind the earthworks. Wave after wave of Abercrombie's men fell beneath the fatal rain of musket fire. And though some of them reached the earthworks despite the murderous volleys, they, too, were driven back.

Abercrombie had hoped this show of courage would turn the tide of battle. It did. For the French.

Nearly two thousand British troops died in that misguided march on Ticonderoga. The French lost only about four hundred men. And even though he still had the superior force and sufficient artillery to crush Montcalm, Abercrombie fled the battlefield.

Duncan Campbell was among the retreating group. And for a while it seemed as if he would triumph over the curse of his kinsman. He hadn't been killed on the day of the battle. He'd only been wounded in the right arm.

But in those days any wound could have severe consequences. Campbell's arm had to be amputated, leading to his death several days later.

He was buried in Union Cemetery near Fort Edward. His tombstone is inscribed:

> *Here Lyes the Body of Duncan*
> *Campbell of Inversaw Esq'*
> *Major To The old Highland*
> *Regt Aged 55 Years Who Died*
> *The 17th July 1758 of The Wounds*
> *He Received In The Attack*
> *of The Retrenchments of*
> *Ticonderoga or Carillon the 8th July 1758*

Duncan Campbell was with his cousin again at last, the two of them now side by side in their final netherlands march.

## The Return of Duncan Campbell

There is an intriguing aftermath to the haunting death of Duncan Campbell.

Though he was buried in America near the site of the battle, the Major of the Highland Regiment returned to Inverawe once again. Like his ghostly kinsman before him, Duncan Campbell's apparition appeared in the castle beside the bed of one of *his* kinsmen.

According to historian Francis Parkman, who cited a letter from James Campbell, the laird of Inverawe at the time he wrote his account, the kinsman was awakened "by some unaccustomed sound, and behold there was a bright light in the room, and he saw a figure, in full Highland regimentals, cross over the room and stoop down over his father's bed and give him a kiss." The son saw the ghostly figure one more time, and in the morning asked his father whose spirit it was.

The father's answer came immediately. It was Duncan Campbell, who returned to the castle in spirit form to tell him that he was killed in a great battle in America.

According to James Campbell's testimony, the spirit appeared on the same day as the battle of Ticonderoga. And though it doesn't have quite the same down-to-earth quality of the rest of the Campbell legend, another family tradition says that two Campbell women saw images of ghostly Highlanders fighting a deadly battle in the sky over the castle right at the moment the laird of Inverawe fell.

## The Province and Provenance of the Campbell Spirit

At the time of Duncan Campbell's first visit from his ghostly kinsman, such events were not totally unheard of in Scotland. Many Highlanders believed in "second sight," in which spirits would visit those who had this gift—or curse—and warn them of danger or death to come. In Lewis Spence's *Encyclopedia of the Occult*, a section on supernatural beliefs in Scotland explains that some Highlanders were reported to possess this skill throughout their lives, while others experienced it only once or twice. Sometimes a spirit came to warn a person about that person's impending death. Other times the apparition was a friend or relative who had recently died. Or sometimes the apparition was the spirit of someone who was actually dying at that very moment.

All these fit in neatly with the fate that befell Major Campbell.

The legend of Duncan Campbell, one of the most haunting incidents in the history of the French and Indian War, has some very persuasive documentation backing it up. The reason the story has persisted for so long is the credibility of those who've written about it. Though there are different accounts available, today the primary source for the story is Francis Parkman, the American historian who reported on Duncan Campbell in an appendix to his 1884 book *Wolfe and Montcalm*. Parkman explained that his account was based on several papers given to him by Dean

Stanley in 1878 along with correspondence from James Campbell himself, the current laird of Inverawe when Parkman wrote his book. Though Parkman was careful to label his account as a legend, he prefaced the tale by writing, "As related by Dean Stanley and approved by Mr. Campbell."

The story is also treated in Frederic Van De Water's 1946 book *Lake Champlain and Lake George*. But one of the most interesting accounts of the incident has been published in booklet form by the Fort Ticonderoga Museum since 1947. This booklet, *Ticonderoga: A Legend of the West Highlands*, reprints Robert Louis Stevenson's poem of the same title, which first appeared in *Scribner's Magazine* in 1887, and includes Parkman's version of the story along with Stevenson's unearthly beautiful epic poem. The museum also keeps in print a number of other publications dealing with the history of Fort Ticonderoga and maintains a collection of manuscripts. The director of the museum association, Nicholas Westbrook, also was a great help in providing correspondence and source material for this chapter.

One of the key questions about the legend of Duncan Campbell is whether or not there is contemporary documentation of the ghostly events. As explained in a letter from Nicholas Westbrook, "Most of the 42nd Highlanders' regimental archives were lost at sea in 1771 during service in Ireland; the balance was captured by Napoleon's troops in 1794. So most primary sources for the regiment's 18th-century history have been lost." Westbrook's letter also mentions another haunting episode in the Duncan Campbell story, concerning other wounded Highlanders who were left behind during the retreat. "A generation later, their shin bones provided tent pegs for Anthony Wayne's Pennsylvania troops garrisoning 'the Ty' during the Revolution."

Another account of the Campbell legend can be found in Jess Stearn's 1963 book *The Door to the Future*, which deals with prophecies and psychics. Stearn adds some details about members of the Fife and Drum Corps of Scotland's Black Watch Regiment who were on a performance tour for Sol Hurok. En route to Montreal, the group detoured to Ticonderoga because they couldn't pass through the region "without seeing where Major Duncan Campbell had given up his ghost."

## A Ghostly Refrain

Fort Ticonderoga finally fell to the British in 1759 when French troops under the command of Captain Hebecourt evacuated as General Amherst led a large British expedition toward the fort. This time the British army maneuvered their artillery into a position from which it could tear down the walls of Ticonderoga.

Captain Hebecourt tried to destroy the fort before he and his troops escaped, but they managed to damage only a part of it. And this time the 42nd Regiment marched victoriously into Ticonderoga along with the 77th Highlanders and other British regulars.

Duncan Campbell could rest easy at the last.

The spirit of Major Campbell is still kept alive more than two hundred years after he fell.

Every year at Ticonderoga the sound of a Highland piper floats through the air during a memorial ceremony performed on the Saturday closest to the July 8 battle. As a lone piper plays, Robert Louis Stevenson's poem is read aloud. The following passages hint at the haunting quality captured by Stevenson:

> This is a tale of the man
>   Who heard a word in the night
> In the land of the heathery hills,
>   In the days of the feud and the fight.
> By the sides of the rainy sea,
>   Where never a stranger came,
> On the awful lips of the dead,
>   He heard the outlandish name.
> It sang in his sleeping ears
>   It hummed in his waking head:
> The name—Ticonderoga,
>   The utterance of the dead.

The masterful poem goes on to recount the ghostly legend of Duncan Campbell, ending with his foretold death at Ticonderoga.

> And far from the hills of heather,
>   Far from the isles of the sea,
> He sleeps in the place of the name
>   As it was doomed to be.

# 13

# The Wraiths of
# Rogers' Rock

## The Unseen Soldiers

Nearly two hundred years after his death, the words of Major Robert Rogers are still widely read—at least by the elite Ranger battalions of the United States Army. The Standing Orders of Major Robert Rogers serve as the introduction to a recent edition of the U.S. Army Ranger Handbook.

During the French and Indian War, Rogers rose through the ranks until he commanded nine companies of Rangers who excelled at scouting and raiding and living in the Adirondack wilderness right next to enemy encampments.

Under Rogers's leadership the Rangers often scouted within earshot of the French troops and allies at Fort Ticonderoga. In fact, on one of his raids, Rogers and his men butchered the livestock of the French troops, took some of them prisoner, and left a note behind for the commander of the fort thanking him for the feast. Frederic

F. Van de Water quotes Rogers's words to Captain Hebecourt in his book *Lake Champlain and Lake George*. "I am obliged to you sir for the rest you have allowed me to take and the fresh meat you have sent me. I shall take good care of my prisoners. My compliments to the Marquis of Montcalm."

As part of a militia from New Hampshire, Rogers's first battle was at a New York site called Bloody Pond, a hellish engagement with French forces on Lake George. At Bloody Pond, Rogers, along with two companies of Rangers, surprised a large force of French and Indians who were looting the bodies of colonials killed in an earlier stage of the battle. With sudden and accurate musket fire, the Rangers decimated the French forces, who fled from the battlefield.

In *Fort William Henry, A History*, Stanley M. Gifford writes: "History tells us that the bodies of the slain were thrown in the small pond near-by and the blood colored the water red, although the setting sun might have had something to do with this illusion . . ."

This ambush followed on the heels of a battle between the regular colonial army and French and Indian allies that raged back and forth through the woods with first one group than the other driven back by ambushes and hand-to-hand fighting. Sudden artillery fire unleashed by the Americans, who'd dragged a cannon through the woods, turned the tide of battle, panicking the French troops and their Abenaki and Iroquois allies and forcing them to withdraw.

It was an auspicious beginning for Rogers, whose legend would soon spread throughout the northern wilderness.

Unlike the British commanders, who favored more traditional engagements, Rogers thrived on skirmishes, ambushes, and sudden hit-and-run raids right into the heart of enemy territory.

As a result of his skill as a woodsman and fighter, Rogers gained a huge following among the American irregulars, hardened men who were eager to clash with the French forces that sallied down from Canada to reinforce their garrisons at Fort Ticonderoga and other strongholds. Like winter wolves loping through the forest, Rogers's Rangers covered great distances on foot or canoe to surprise and overwhelm superior forces before vanishing back into the woods.

## The Haunted Hunters

Like many other Rangers, Rogers took part in the campaign against Fort Ticonderoga where Duncan Campbell, the haunted Highlander, fell in battle just as his ghostly kinsman in Scotland had predicted.

Rogers also had a brush with the supernatural—or at least so goes the legend.

In March of 1758, while leading a raiding party of two hundred Rangers from Fort Edward through heavy snow, Rogers and his men ran into a force of French-allied Indians nearly a hundred strong. The Rangers killed about half of them and then pursued the fleeing Indians—right into a French army that was on the move. Outnumbered by nearly five hundred men in the ensuing battle, the Rangers were gradually overcome and scattered throughout the woods, where they were hunted down by Indian scouting parties.

In his 1896 collection of history and folklore, *Myths and Legends of Our Own Land*, Charles Skinner writes about the legend of Rogers's escape. A band of Indians pursued Rogers to a site later named Rogers' Rock or Rogers' Slide, "a lofty precipice at the lower end of Lake George."

At the brink of the rock, Rogers threw his pack down to the ice-covered lake below to make it look like he'd gone over the edge, then reversed his snowshoes and traced his footsteps back down the way he'd climbed. He vanished into the woods before the trackers caught up to him. "Seeing that his shoe-marks led to the rock, while none pointed back, they concluded that he had flung himself off and committed suicide to avoid capture."

But a short time later, they saw him far out on the ice where he soon would be out of their range. According to Skinner's version of the story, the Indians held the site in superstitious regard and "attributed his preservation to the Great Spirit and forebore to fire on him . . . believing that spirits haunted the wood and hurled bad souls down the cliff." Cloaked in the safety of superstition, Rogers was able to meet up with a rescue party from Fort Edward.

Van de Water also writes about this incident but treats it in a more skeptical manner, in the belief that Rogers himself would have told the tale often and widely. So, looking at the incident from a skeptical point of view, the woods were haunted only by the freshly departed souls of the Rangers who were killed by the pursuing French and Indians.

Only about one-fourth of Rogers's Rangers made it back to Fort Edward from the raid.

The story of Rogers's miraculous escape has persisted throughout the years, along with the much more documented events in the life of the founder of the Rangers. His name is still well known in the area and in the history books—and in many ways his presence can still be felt in Lake George.

Cannons and muskets still roar from the ramparts of Fort William Henry where the Rangers were quartered. And Indian, redcoat, and Ranger walk around the ramparts—as part of regular exhibitions held at the fort and museum. During the usual exhibition only a single musket shot is fired, but it booms loud and clear and echoes across the glassy lake—a distant hint of the deafening roar that sounded back in the days when Rangers haunted the woods.

# 14

# The Valley Forge Vision

### The Spirit of 1777

The spirit of America hovered over the frigid ground of Valley Forge, blown this way and that by the changing winds of war that swept across the newly independent country.

It was a time when lives were at stake every day, when the fate of a country hung in a delicate balance. A time when men with vision stepped forward—and when visions descended.

Though the history of the Revolutionary War is well known, there's another history at work here. A secret history with a phantomlike provenance.

The well-known incident in which, as a young boy, Washington supposedly confessed to chopping down a cherry tree because he couldn't tell a lie was a ghost of Parson Weems's imagination. Facts were flexible in the hands of the good parson, who made his living as a pastor, bookseller, and author. As far as Weems was concerned, if it made a good story it became part of history. As a result, his biography of Washington has a carnival aura about it, full of brightly spun anecdotes that decorate the truth hidden somewhere off the midway.

Along with the cherry tree, Mason Weems conjured up a story of George Washington kneeling in the snow in winter and praying to God for guidance. This tale was repeated so often that it not only became part of written history, but painters have made stirring portraits to commemorate the occasion.

But even Weems's imagination is no match for the story about the Valley Forge vision of Washington that originated several decades after his death.

According to the story, Washington was overcome with despair because of the hardships his army was suffering in winter camp at Valley Forge. Since General Washington was the one man whose vision kept the army together, if *he* gave up hope the army would crumble.

Fortunately, hope came to him.

It came to him in the form of a beautiful angel who suddenly materialized in his room. The celestial messenger shimmered in the candlelight and with a majestic wave of her hand enveloped the room with a strange mist.

From out of the mist a panoramic vision unfolded, showing the different countries of the world under a cloud of warfare and darkness. Washington saw endless armies rising and falling, and towns and cities springing up only to be reduced to ashes. But then the cities grew again and the cycle repeated itself. As Washington watched in a trancelike state, the angel spoke in somber tones, saying, "Son of the Republic, look and learn."

The startled general was treated to a living tableau of war and revival, of an American civilization growing from the great struggles it faced. First there was the war Washington had to fight. Then the Civil War. Then, finally, an ultimate war in which all the armies of the world marched against America, only to be defeated by the American spirit—and an army of spirits that came down from the heavens to fight alongside the Americans.

After cautioning Washington that every person in America must fight for God and the Union, the angel vanished.

And Washington's shaken faith was renewed.

The Union was saved.

Or so the story goes.


To a modern sensibility the Valley Forge vision seems almost like a film projected on the walls of the commander-in-chief's quarters by a celestial time traveler.

But to the public at the time the "vision" first made the rounds, the fantastic story was most welcome. This biblical tableau seemed to enforce the high esteem and near worship in which Washington was held. Considering his astonishing feat of holding the country together when other men would have let it fall, why couldn't a vision have played a part?

Specters *were* hovering over the brittle spirits of the American troops quartered in the desolate camp at Valley

Forge. The specters of famine, sickness, and death from exposure. Shortly after they set up camp, Washington declared more than one quarter of the eleven thousand troops at Valley Forge unfit for duty.

In that winter of 1777 many of the men often went without food, winter clothes, or even shoes for their bare feet that left bloody tracks in the snow. Although Congress had gathered stores of food and clothing for Washington's men, there was no organized transportation to get it to them.

Though many scholars have questioned Washington's military skills, there is no doubt he was the undisputed leader of the colonial forces. Just over six feet tall, strong and wiry all his life, he was the kind of man others would follow. Frontiersmen and officers alike saw a sense of purpose and command in him, a moral vision that was lacking in other generals with more glorious victories attached to their names.

Without Washington there would have been no lasting army at Valley Forge. The ragged troops clustered around him would have splintered into broken shards and melted away long before spring. He, the American spirit personified, held them together.

What made the long winter doubly hard to contend with was the fact that less than twenty miles away the British army was comfortably quartered in Philadelphia, taking advantage of the plentiful supplies sold to them by shopkeepers who often refused to deal with Washington's army.

Other enemies Washington faced could be found among

rival officers in New York who plotted and schemed to replace him as commander-in-chief with General Horatio Gates. Chief among the plotters was a General Conway, an Irish soldier who made it a personal war to attack Washington's competence at every chance.

But Washington survived the push to replace him, just as he and his men survived the winter at Valley Forge.

And there were some benefits to be found in the wintry encampment. By the time the nearly eleven-thousand-strong army left camp in the spring, there was a bond between them that had been forged by the unending adversity. And the army that marched out of Valley Forge was not the same that marched into it. Throughout the winter Baron von Steuben, a German military man sympathetic to Washington's cause, had helped organize and train the ragtag army into a professional force that could hold its own against the British troops.

Washington also accepted the help of Marquis de Lafayette, whose position in French society and whose diplomatic skills were perhaps greater than any military help he could offer. The ties with France grew steadily stronger until, as spring arrived at Valley Forge, the French allied themselves with the Americans and brought their superior naval power to bear upon the British.

So it appears that throughout that long cold winter, military, political, and spiritual bonds were formed.

While the military details are well known, the veracity of the spiritual aid is still up in the air. Washington may well have had visions, but it's hard to establish whether an angel ever marched to Valley Forge.

## The Province of Angels

The story of the Valley Forge vision has grown throughout the years, with more and more "details" added with each telling. It appears often in collections of ghost stories, many of the writers treating it as undisputable fact without ever mentioning the source.

But Neal Wilgus's thought-provoking and thoroughly researched book *The Illuminoids*, a history of popular and lesser-known conspiracies and legends, traces the Valley Forge vision to an article by Wesley Bradshaw written in the 1860s and published in *The National Tribune* in 1880. Wilgus mentions other places where the story was printed, including a 1950 edition of *Stars and Stripes*. He also explains that Bradshaw's article was based on the recollection of a man named Anthony Sherman, who allegedly was stationed at Valley Forge.

## A Matter of Fact

It is hard to pin down legends surrounding great men or events and say whether they are mythical or not.

But a story like the Valley Forge vision, if true, should have circulated widely before one man in his nineties came forward to tell it to a newspaperman. Word of such a breathtaking vision would certainly have made the rounds of the encampment and appeared in journals and letters and spread by word of mouth when the soldiers returned home.

After reading several versions of the vision at Valley Forge, I searched through many of Washington's writings as well as documents about Washington and saw no mention of it. I then sought the opinions of some Washington scholars.

Phil Chase, an editor of *The Washington Papers* based at the University of Virginia, is working on a long-range project that will print documents not well known to the public, including not only Washington's letters but the responses to them—in order to show both sides of the issues. The project involves a series of volumes, some already published and several more to come. Eventually, the entire *Washington Papers* will be placed on disk so they'll be readily available to the public.

With such a wealth of documents on hand, if anyone would know about a vision at Valley Forge, it would be Phil Chase. But there was no such vision mentioned in any of *The Washington Papers*.

Though Phil Chase has heard of the story about Washington's vision, he believes the legend was a part of a nineteenth-century trend to project religious and patriotic views onto historical figures from another era.

If the story of the vision is true, then the details should certainly be floating in the air of Valley Forge, Pennsylvania. From 1893 to 1976, the site of Washington's encampment was a state park. In 1976, it became the Valley Forge National Historical Park.

I contacted Joan Dutcher, the official historian at the

National Park, to see what her opinion was on the Valley Forge vision. Quite familiar with the newspaper account that appeared in the late 1800s, Dutcher believes that it's a good story—but only a story. Like many other legends that arose around George Washington, such as his fabled felling of a cherry tree in his father's orchard, it took on a life of its own and far outdistanced the facts.

And so, in the end, Washington's vision seems to belong to the realm of legend rather than fact. But it has taken on such a well-detailed aura that it still haunts the pages of history.

And who's to say that Washington didn't have a private vision of his own? A more down-to-earth vision of leading a country through the pangs of birth into true independence, a vision now shared by millions of people.

# 15

## God's Mad Gunman

### The Misguided Messiah

As the well-dressed former Army general walked through the passenger terminal at the Baltimore and Potomac railroad station in Washington, D.C., preparing to board a train for New York, a slender and sallow-complexioned man in a slouch hat rushed toward him. The man was about to embark on a divine mission, flying on the wings of madness.

He took out a bulldog revolver loaded with five .44-caliber bullets.

He'd bought the gun for the sum of eleven dollars. Though he'd practiced with it until he considered himself a marksman, military skills were not required for what he was about to do.

He fired twice at point-blank range.

And while the shots echoed in the railroad station, President James A. Garfield dropped to the floor, blood pouring from two massive wounds.

It was July 2, 1881, a few months into Garfield's term of office.

Garfield had survived four years in the Civil War as the youngest general in the Union Army. He had survived the tumultuous politics of an era that often turned the White House into a madhouse.

But he would not survive the bullets of a madman, a would-be cabinet member whose most effective campaigns were waged inside the deranged corridors of his mind, a man who just a short time before had been speaking to near-empty halls while urgently preparing the world for the Second Coming of Christ.

The assassin, Charles J. Guiteau, was, in his own words, "a lawyer, a theologian, and a politician."

And he failed at all three.

Unfortunately, he succeeded at taking the life of President Garfield, who, at age fifty-six, was still a down-to-earth Lincolnesque lawyer and military man whose sense of humor often put him at odds with the somber saber-rattlers of the D.C. political machines.

Throughout the eighty days before Garfield succumbed to his wounds, his physicians often hinted at a full recovery. But ultimately Garfield would fall to the gun of the misguided messiah, a man who carried a letter of intent with him on the day of the assassination. Like several other newspapers of the day, *The New York Times* printed the letter in their Sunday, July 3, edition. In it Guiteau offers some of his cracked cosmology:

". . . Life is a flimsy dream, and it matters little when one goes . . . I presume the President was a Christian and that he will be happier in Paradise than here."

In what he presumes to be a lawyerly brief explaining why this had to come to pass, Guiteau continues in a pompous rant. "His death was a political necessity. I am a lawyer, a theologian, and a politician . . . I am a Stalwart of the Stalwarts."

This letter and a later lengthy statement show Guiteau's exaggerated sense of self-importance and hint at the wonderful world he thought he would usher in. Rather than being punished, he fully expected to become a prominent member in Vice-President Chester A. Arthur's circle when Arthur assumed the presidency. In Guiteau's twisted logic, since he paved the way for Arthur by killing Garfield, the new president would be most grateful.

Several times after his arrest, Guiteau referred to Arthur as his good friend. He repeatedly mentioned the names of generals and influential politicians as close intimates who soon would be in position to take his advice.

First, of course, they would have to free him. That would come in time, he thought, when the world at large realized what a hero he was. Never mind the fact that he was a murderer. After all, he was running on a higher platform, endorsed by God himself.

Apparently, those divine plans didn't encompass his escape. Guiteau was captured immediately after the assassination attempt by a police officer who plucked the bizarrely dressed man from a crowd he'd tried to hide in. From there he was taken to a Washington, D.C., jail where he expected to hold court and distribute copies of his proposal to reform America, a madman's version of the State of the Union address.

Guiteau was so sure of his eventual release and reward that he attempted to bestow his patronage on one of the detectives questioning him. Guiteau promised that he would use his influence to make him the chief of police.

## A Conspiracy of One

By the time he was thirty-six, Charles Guiteau had built up an image of himself as a man of greatness, a man whose intellect and force of will were destined to make him a leader of men. It was not an image shared by anyone else.

In newspaper accounts of the time, his creditors often referred to him as a deadbeat.

Critics who took the time to sift through his religious writings found them to be singularly disjointed. Side by side with established religious teachings, his unfounded gospels were incomprehensible to his audience. And so the longed-for disciples never flocked to his banner.

As with most assassination attempts, there were rumors of an organized conspiracy. But the only conspirators seem to have been the diminished personalities of Charles Guiteau—the lawyer, the theologian, the politician. Even so, a dispatch from Washington was carried in *The New York Times* on July 3, 1881, that raised the possibility of a wider net of conspirators:

"Attorney General MacVeagh has been in consultation

tonight with members of the detective force and his confidential agents, who are working on the criminal features of this case. One of the leading members of this branch of the tragedy says that the assassin had confederates. This fact, he claims, is established beyond a doubt . . . It is asserted that the murderer was signaled by a confederate of the approach of the President's carriage.''

Another theory proposed the existence of a "Star Route" conspiracy. President Garfield had recently begun to crack down on a group of senators, postmasters, and private contractors who were swindling the public on a massive scale. At the time there were many mail routes, known as Star Routes, spread out across the country that couldn't be reached by railcar or boat. Contracts for the delivery of mail to these locations were awarded to private companies. Following their instincts, some of the politicians handing out the contracts rigged a system of kickbacks and payoffs that overcharged the government and often billed it for work and routes that didn't exist.

Garfield made a lot of enemies and ruined a lot of careers when he exposed the corruption in the system, causing some alarmist writers to suggest that the assassination attempt was a revenge killing.

This conspiracy idea fell back into the realm of fantasy when subsequent investigation revealed that Guiteau was the disturbed brain behind the operation. As he claimed, his only accomplice was Almighty God, or, as he often called him, "The Lordy."

Guiteau acted alone—perhaps because he couldn't bear to have anyone else share in the expected glory. Nor was he the type able to enlist others to his cause. In fact, an anticharisma was at work with Guiteau. To anyone who listened to his religious or political views, it quickly became apparent that he was a lunatic.

Even before he attacked Garfield, the White House guards had concluded that Guiteau was insane. A Detective McElfresh of the District Police, while gathering information on the assassin, discovered that "Guiteau has been noticed lounging about the White House . . . He was regarded as a harmless lunatic." The guards frequently chased him off the grounds whenever he tried to enter the White House, which he considered his future home.

But Guiteau wasn't so harmless, according to those who lived with him. His sister recalled that at one time she believed Guiteau was about to kill her while he was in a trancelike state.

Before she divorced him, Guiteau's wife, Anne Bunn, was frequently battered and abused, and there were reports of similar treatment of prostitutes he frequented. After all, he believed himself to be a godlike entity and anyone who dared to make him mad deserving of punishment at his hands. He delivered frightening rants to creditors and anyone who dared dispute his bizarre philosophies of life.

Because of his embezzling nature and his refusal to deal with people he owed money to, Guiteau was described by one reporter of the time as "a half crazed pettifogging lawyer who has been an unsuccessful applicant for office under the Government."

His brother-in-law, George Scoville, made a lengthy

statement to the courts about Guiteau's mental state, reporting that Guiteau had previously been judged insane by a number of physicians, though he seldom was kept in asylums for long.

Once again, he was thought to be harmless.

According to Scoville's statement, "His insanity consisted for the great part in imagining himself some great personage . . . He wrote a book and delivered a number of lectures on the Second Coming of Christ."

In light of his crazed state, one wonders if the subject of the book was Guiteau himself, and the book a bible for his impending reign on earth.

Reporting on his jailhouse conversation with Guiteau, Scoville said, "I asked him the direct question how it happened that he undertook this sad business . . . He said, 'It came to me first as a revelation from God, while I was in bed . . . It came as a revelation to me that I should kill Mr. Garfield and end the difficulties existing in the Republican Party.' "

The assassin's brother, John Wilson Guiteau, was a successful lawyer who attributed the murderous deed to Charles Guiteau's political aspirations. "I knew that my brother had been for years insane to a certain degree. I supposed . . . that he had committed the act in a moment of wild frenzy, under the hallucination excited by the failure of his crazy attempts to get an office."

In fact, Guiteau had previously contacted President Garfield, requesting a position in the government. His only basis for seeking such high office was the divine right of madmen. He had carefully scripted unwanted campaign literature for Garfield, and no doubt felt he had contributed to his election.

Another man who was convinced that Guiteau was a dangerous individual was Congressman Carter H. Harrison, who several years earlier had been given detailed architectural plans by Guiteau for a huge national park that would erect monuments to the great men of history, past, present, and future. There's little doubt that Guiteau imagined that he, too, would one day be idolized in that monumental park for his contributions to society.

Initially, the plan was in the realm of the rational. But then Guiteau informed the congressman that he had a secret technology at his disposal, a process that would make the statues harder than any metal known to man.

Harrison returned the plans to the madman.

And the madman accused him of stealing the secrets of his technology, holding back some crucial diagrams he needed to make that technology effective. From then on he harassed the congressman, adding one more member to the imagined conspiracy against *him*.

In Guiteau's tortured mind, the greatest scoundrel was still President Garfield, who was guilty of not following Guiteau's advice when it came to political matters. The respect that Garfield had from the public was something that Guiteau craved himself, something that he felt he deserved.

But the two men were worlds apart.

Much like Lincoln, Garfield was born in a log cabin on the frontier. He became a riverboat worker, a scholar and teacher, a preacher, university president, and soldier. By the age of thirty-six he had risen to the rank of general, and after fighting in the Civil War began a lengthy career in politics—a career ended when he achieved the presidency and a madman took it away from him.

Guiteau's life had been one of manic delusion. The would-be orator, theologian, and lawyer believed he was destined to shape the world. He also wrote political speeches that no one wanted to hear, which turned out to be incomprehensible instead of eloquent. Despite his claim to greatness, Guiteau made his living by collecting debts. And according to many of his clients, he misappropriated the funds for himself, just as he tried to appropriate the accomplishments of men such as Garfield.

## Assassins in Bloom

The spirit of assassination drifted upon the Potomac in a malevolent fog that year. For Charles Guiteau was not the only assassin receiving otherworldly inspiration.

On July 5, 1881, two days after Guiteau shot the president, an army veteran named David McNamara arrived at police headquarters in Washington, D.C. McNamara carried a revolver with him into the police station and calmly explained that God had inspired him to kill Secretary of State James G. Blaine . . . or Chester A. Arthur. McNamara wasn't quite sure whom he was supposed to kill. Apparently, his revelation wasn't as specific as Guiteau's. He just knew he had to kill somebody important.

He told the officials that previously he'd been instructed to kill President Grant but had failed in that.

The most curious thing McNamara did that day was offer to instruct the authorities on how these spirits worked—possibly so they would know what targets to protect from the "inspired" assassins. McNamara, like Guiteau, had also spent time in an insane asylum. He'd been discharged from a Philadelphia asylum in January.

Fortunately, there was a method to his madness, and McNamara knew his revelations were evil rather than inspired.

## The Final Sentence

Right up to the end, Charles Guiteau made blustering pronouncements that treated the world to his bizarre views. Throughout his lengthy trial he preached and harangued witnesses, lawyers, and the judge hearing his case. He had found a worldwide audience at last who appeared to hang on his every word. Newspaper reporters found him a steady source of copy. The public was intrigued by the demented man who held congress with God. Letters with checks for his defense fund poured in, so much so that he began to scold some of the donors, saying, "I don't want anyone to send worthless checks. The checks should be to my order. Anyone can send money."

But despite the money, despite the moral outrage of Guiteau that he was being tried for a crime, the trial proceeded as expected. The testimony of physicians, witnesses, and acquaintances was remarkably alike.

An Associated Press article that appeared in the *Schenectady Daily Union* on December 12, 1881, captured the prevailing sentiment. Referring to Dr. Charles Spitzka, a witness for the defense, the newspaper report said, "The witness examined the prisoner in the jail yesterday and was satisfied that he is insane."

Guiteau didn't see it that way. In his mind he wasn't totally insane, although he allowed as how others may perceive his divinely inspired act as such. As he had argued to Judge Cox on January 17, he expected that an acquittal was in order. "That if the jury believe it was right to remove the President because I had special divine authority so to do and was forced to do it by the deity, they will acquit on the ground of transitory mania." And though he called upon God as his witness, no such testimony was entered into the trial.

Despite his theatrics and hopes of celestial intervention, Guiteau was eventually convicted for the murder of President Garfield. He was scheduled to be hanged on June 30, 1882.

On the day of the hanging his brother John said, "His life is a wreck, worthless, and I think this is a most fitting end to a checkered insane career."

As one of his last missives to mankind, Guiteau wrote a farewell address and a message to God which he would shortly be able to deliver in person. Practically every newspaper of the day carried the message, giving Guiteau the forum he'd sought for so long: "Father now I go to thee and the Savior. I have finished the work Thou gavest me to do . . . The world does not yet appreciate my mission, but Thou knowest it . . . The diabolical spirit of this nation, its government and its newspapers toward me will justify Thee in cursing them. . . . Farewell ye men of earth . . ."

On the scaffold just before his hanging, Guiteau told the audience that he'd written a prayer—which they could set to music in the future, perhaps thinking it would be an eternal anthem sung forever in America: "I am going to the Lordy, I am so glad . . . I saved my party and my land . . . Glory Hallelujah, I am with Lordy!"

A short time later, he received the applause he'd sought in all of his incarnations.

A newspaper reporter recounted the scene. "Instantly the spring was touched. The drop fell at 12:40. Guiteau swung around in the air. His body was turned partly around . . . Thousands of people outside hurrahed lustily . . ."

Charles J. Guiteau, "lawyer, theologian, and politician," had gone to meet his maker.

# 16

## Invisible Invasions

### Worlds' War One

The first documented battle between the forces of Earth and invaders from Mars occurred on October 30, 1938.

At 8:00 that night, millions of Americans heard about the invasion from an increasingly frantic number of bulletins that interrupted a popular radio broadcast on the Columbia Broadcasting System.

As word of the arrival of the Martians spread across the country, panic set in, especially in New Jersey and New York—the areas closest to the reported invasion.

Grovers Mill, New Jersey, was hardest hit.

That was where the strange ships of the Martians buried into the ground on impact, then gradually opened up like metal egg shells to unleash the strange-looking, bloodsucking monsters. These terrifying Martians attacked the citizens of Earth with their hideous tentacles, insidious death rays and mists of poisonous gas.

As the breathless announcers on the show reported, the United States Army and the police were unable to stop the Martians. No weapon had any effect on them.

The only thing earthlings could do was run for their lives.

And run they did.

As reported in *The New York Times* on the days immediately after the broadcast, many roads were clogged with people trying to drive out of town and escape the Martians. Phone lines were jammed as alarmed citizens called the police to find out what was happening, or called their friends and relatives to warn them of the invasion.

The "invasion" that so many people believed in was actually a radio broadcast of the Mercury Theatre of the Air on the Columbia Broadcasting System from their New York studio. It was a radio dramatization of H. G. Wells's classic 1897 novel *War of the Worlds*, in which technologically superior Martians send an armada of spaceships to Earth.

The radio play, developed by Howard Koch and Orson Welles, ingeniously transported the scene of the invasion from England to the United States and set it against a backdrop of a Park Plaza ballroom that featured the music of Ramon Raquello and his orchestra.

As the music played, the announcers began cutting in with bulletins about strange explosions seen on the surface of Mars. After the host returned to the ballroom for more music, additional bulletins came in, featuring astronomers, scientists, and military men who gave their learned commentary about the arrival of interplanetary vehicles.

Eventually the show was taken over by one news report after another that featured a frightening scenario of invasion and conquest, as everything Earth threw against the Martians failed miserably.

What made the invasion seem so real, of course, was the artistry of Orson Welles and his troupe of veteran radio actors.

At the time, radio was the main source of entertainment and information for a large number of the American population. An innate trust had been built up between listeners and newsmen. So when the fictitious newsmen apparently cut into the musical broadcast, many of the listeners were conditioned to believe what they heard.

In *The Invasion from Mars*, Hadley Cantrill's 1940 study of the widespread panic caused by the radio broadcast, the author quotes people from all walks of life who actually believed the invasion was occurring exactly as stated by the radio announcers. Out of an audience estimated at six million listeners, almost one million were upset by the broadcast, many of them fearing for their lives.

The day following the broadcast, October 31, 1938, the *New York Times* headline read:

RADIO LISTENERS IN PANIC, TAKING WAR DRAMA AS FACT. *Many Flee Homes to Escape 'Gas Raid From Mars'—Phone Calls Swamp Police at Broadcast of Wells Fantasy*

The accompanying article confirmed what many authorities had known the night before: "The broadcast, which disrupted households, interrupted religious services, created traffic jams and clogged communications systems, was made by Orson Welles . . . At least a score of adults required medical treatment for shock and hysteria." The paper also carried the announcements made by New York and New Jersey State Police, informing the public that the invasion was imaginary, a fictitious broadcast that was no cause for alarm.

As a result of the hysteria caused by the broadcast, Orson Welles and the Columbia Broadcasting System made public apologies for any hysteria they caused.

Since then, to prevent such a widescale case of hysteria from recurring, the Federal Communications Commission has kept a tighter rein over what can go over the air. As recently as 1992, the FCC approved fines of up to $25,000 for any broadcast hoax that alarms the public and causes civil and federal authorities to respond to imaginary crises dreamed up by the broadcasters.

Though many people were critical of Orson Welles for his role in creating such a wave of hysteria, the fact that so many people believed in the invasion was a testament to his artistry.

The broadcast also served as a testament to the power of the FCC. Though the army and the police failed in their efforts to stop the marauding Martians, the FCC was able to step in at the hour of need and save the world from all future invasions—at least those on the airwaves.

## Other Invasions

Though the War of the Worlds was the most prominent invasion from otherworldly forces, it was not the first.

During World War I, hundreds of British and Germans reported seeing angels and phantom bowmen at the Battle of Mons—an apparent hoax dreamed up after the fact by Arthur Machen, who wrote a "news account" of the divine interference for the *London Daily Telegraph*.

Called "The Bowmen," the story was widely circulated throughout England when a number of returning soldiers testified that the events in Machen's fiction piece actually reflected what they'd seen on the battlefield.

Another World War I invisible "invasion" occurred when rumors spread across England, France, and Germany that a large army of Russian cossacks was mobilizing in the north of England for an attack on Germany. Though no one had actually seen the cossacks, many soldiers on both sides of the conflict believed they existed, and as a result, these invisible soldiers spread their fair share of terror through the German ranks.

An invisible invasion even occurred back in 1692 during King Philip's War when American colonists in Massachusetts felt themselves besieged by a ghostly force of French and Indian warriors. The sound of horse hoofs clopping on country lanes was heard all throughout Gloucester and Plymouth. Ghostly Indians were seen prowling in the mist, and their war cries echoed up and down the countryside.

As Charles Skinner wrote in his 1896 book *Myths and Legends of Our Own Land*, the colonists came to believe that "These were not an enemy of flesh and blood, but devils who hoped to work a moral perversion of the colony."

Beset by such evil forces, the colonists rallied behind Ebenezer Babson and Richard Dolliver, who led forays against the ghostly horde known as "the specter leaguers." With a combination of buckshot and common prayer, these brave colonists exorcised the ghost guard that had descended upon them—putting an end once and for all to the devils' brigade that had besieged Gloucester.

# 17

## The General
## Strikes Twice

### The Timeless Warrior

When he was a Roman legionnaire in Gaul, George S. Patton served under Julius Caesar. During several more lifetimes he was always a military man, whether it was horseman, Highlander, or trooper.

Throughout these campaigns Patton gained experience and grew in stature until finally, at the end of World War II, he was known around the world as "Blood and Guts" Patton, a man who'd fought on three continents and come out a victor on each one.

General Patton made no secret of his belief in reincarnation. In fact, he was quite precise about his past lives and his belief in telepathy, according to his biographer, Martin Blumenson, in *Patton: The Man Behind the Legend 1885–1945*.

Patton's own book about his career, *War as I Knew It*, contains some hints about his martial and mystical beliefs, and a poem he wrote in 1944 called "Through a Glass Darkly" also expresses his belief in reincarnation.

The incidents that tell of his past lives began in World War I when he arrived in France after fighting in General Pershing's campaign against Pancho Villa. When he served in Mexico Patton was a second lieutenant, a cavalryman known for his independence and willingness to take risks.

Now that he was in France, Patton was tasked with forming a tank corps headquartered in Langres. The site happened to be near Roman ruins that dated to the time of Caesar. The Romans had built several roads that stretched out from the fortress down into the surrounding countryside, concrete arteries for its legionnaires to pour into the heart of France.

A medieval air still hangs over the town of Langres, with its gates and towers and ramparts. This mountainous aerie provided a clear view of the Marne River and from ancient days had been a military stronghold. As it was once again in December 1917 when Patton entered the medieval town.

Such a heady atmosphere would have an effect on anyone, but on a man like Patton, who had strong martial and mystical leanings, it had a profound effect.

According to the popular version of the story, upon arriving at Langres, Patton declined a tour of the area because he was already familiar with the town—from a previous lifetime when he'd fought there in Roman armor.

Since Patton had always considered himself part of a mystical and martial bloodline, the incident at Langres is often written about as a factual episode pointing out his belief in reincarnation. But in *The Man Behind the Legend*, Blumenson writes that this particular instance is a bit of embroidered history, calling it "a later and apocryphal story told of Patton's arrival at night during a rainstorm."

But there *were* other cases that demonstrated Patton's belief in reincarnation.

## The Roman Legion of George Patton

In *War as I Knew It*, Patton's own reflections on his military career—primarily for the years 1942 to 1945—he occasionally shows a mystical bent. But only in passing. Most of the book is down to earth, containing diary entries, reports, observations on military life and tactics. It also shows his sardonic humor from time to time and his battle philosophy.

For example, on the matter of bridges Patton wrote, "In river crossings, all bridges must be one way—toward the enemy—until the situation has steadied." He also urged rapid decisions and attacks, rather than long, drawn-out logistics: ". . . A good plan violently executed *now* is better than a perfect plan next week."

This is the philosophy that got him and the Third Army into battle much faster than others considered possible, even the Germans. Patton's rapid deployment of his troops brought him into position to contain the German advance at the Battle of the Bulge, and it helped him cross the Rhine before his longtime British competitor Montgomery.

It was at the Rhine that Patton exhibited some actions that cause many to think he was "re-creating" an incident from a previous lifetime. In the company of three other officers, Patton crossed the Rhine on March 24, 1945, and walked in the footsteps of conquerors before him.

"When we got to the far side," he wrote, "I also deliberately stubbed my toe and fell, picking up a handful of German soil, in emulation of Scipio Africanus and William the Conqueror, who both stumbled and both made a joke of it, saying 'I see in my hands the soil of Africa' or '. . . the soil of England.' I saw in my hands the soil of Germany."

Scipio Africanus was the Roman general who, like Patton, was sent to Africa to do battle in Carthage. Scipio defeated Hannibal, while Patton's troops helped eliminate the German presence in Tunisia. And, of course, to Patton the two may have been one and the same.

Another episode occurred in Trier during World War II. Trier was also a strategic crossroads that had been the site of battle from the days of the Romans. Here in the Amphitheater gladiators fought in mortal combat before crowds of up to twenty thousand people. Adding to the glories of the past was the fact that the Emperor Constantine had made Trier an imperial residence.

Writing about his visit in *this* lifetime to the site, Patton said, "The Roman legions marching on Trier from Luxembourg used this same road, and one could almost smell the coppery sweat and see the low dust clouds where those stark fighters moved forward into battle.''

Still standing was the huge Roman gate, turned black from age, that served as the ancient gateway to Trier, a city Patton occupied for yet another time. This is one of the incidents corroborated by Blumenson, who wrote that Patton was ''so sure of his previous presence there.''

Aside from his belief that he had visited these places in other lifetimes, Patton depended a good deal upon his intuition. In one passage in *War as I Knew It*, he explains how his ''sixth sense'' came into play at a strategic moment that turned the tide of battle. When the 87th Infantry and the 11th Army Division arrived at Neufchateau near dawn instead of the night before as scheduled, an imminent Allied attack was about to be postponed because the troops had been on the move throughout the night.

''General Middleton requested a delay of one day in the attack,'' Patton wrote. ''I demanded that he attack anyway that morning, because my sixth sense told me it was vital.''

Apparently, Patton's sixth sense was right on target, because Middleton's attacking force ran straight into the flank of almost three divisions of Germans who had just launched a surprise counteroffensive. ''Had my divisions delayed one day, the German counter-attack might well have cut off the tenuous corridor we had been able to establish from Arlon to Bastogne.''

Earlier Patton writes of an incident that seems reminiscent of a hundred war movies in which the commanders advance in a hail of lead without getting touched. During the Meuse-Argonne Offensive, a nest of German machine gunners stopped members of the 301st Brigade who were digging a breach through German trenches.

Under the onslaught, the crews stopped digging and sought cover. At this point Patton advanced to the killing zone. "In order to restore confidence, Captain English and myself stood on top of the parapet. This persuaded the men to resume their digging. Strange to say, several of the men were hit, but neither of us was touched."

And so while machine gunners felled men all around him, Patton remained safe. It seemed that as long as he was in the middle of a fight, the gods of war were protecting him. It was only after the war's end—when his great campaign was over—that he was hurt in a jeep accident that ultimately caused his death.

Patton's closing words in his memoir seem almost prophetic: "It is rather sad for me to think that my last opportunity for earning my pay has passed. At least, I have done my best as God gave me the chance."

## Patton's Phantom Force

With his mystical background, it's appropriate that General Patton was chosen as the man to lead a ghost army in battle.

As part of the deception foisted upon the Germans regarding the intended location of the D-Day Invasion, Patton was given command of a ghost army called the First

U.S. Army Group. Known as FUSAG, it was tasked with leading the massive invasion to the shores of France—at Pas de Calais.

The army existed primarily on paper, but the Germans prepared to meet it at Calais anyway, convinced by carefully leaked radio messages that troops were gathering across the English Channel and were being supplied with everything they needed to launch the invasion. Artfully worked double agents also provided Hitler with information that the invasion would come at Pas de Calais.

As a result of the ghostly movements of Patton's First Army Group, the Germans diverted troops and tanks to defend the strategic port, rather than add them to their defenses at the real target of Normandy.

## Through a Glass Darkly

In many ways Patton lived up to the ideal of a warrior bard of old. Not just a general, but a scholar. A poet. Like Druidic bards whose epics of their chieftains in battle were based on first-person observation—and participation— Patton was also a writer. While many critics might say that if Patton had the heart of a literary man it was only for breakfast, in reality he had a remarkable gift for chronicling the military spirit.

One of George Patton's poems, "Through a Glass Darkly," delivered most eloquently by George C. Scott in the film *Patton*, directly addresses his thoughts on reincarnation.

# 18

## The History of
## the Future

### Poetic Justice

Edgar Allan Poe created some of the most mysterious fiction pieces of his time. He also created a particularly macabre work of fiction that actually happened years after his story was published.

In *The Narrative of Arthur Gordon Pym*, Poe wrote about a journey beyond the known boundaries of earth. One of the characters in the story, Richard Parker, met a gruesome fate that stuck in the minds of the readers of Poe's story.

The story, originally printed as part of a newspaper serial, got a second life when a real-life person named Richard Parker met exactly the same fate as Poe's character.

Considering his affinity with the metaphysical realm—as shown in his stunning fiction and poetry—it seems most fitting that Poe was actually writing a history of the future in his short story.

In some respects, Poe lived the life of a doomed character who would have been at home in one of his short stories.

Orphaned as a young boy, Poe was adopted by a well-to-do family only to have his adoptive mother die while he was still a young man. Later on in life, when his reputation as a poet and short-story writer was growing strong, he married a young woman named Virginia. Unfortunately, she died of tuberculosis about ten years later.

In an attempt to drown his sorrows, Poe took to drink and died a few years later in 1849 in the streets of Baltimore, out of his mind and collapsing from exhaustion. A number of writers from the period guessed that Poe was a victim of one of the crooked voting schemes of the time—in which "voters" were kept in a drunken or drugged state and shepherded by political goons and hacks from place to place to vote over and over. As a result, Poe came to a tragic and pitiful end, just like one of his mad narrators.

While Poe is known for his horror tales and his moody and striking poems like "The Raven," he's credited with developing the modern detective story in "The Murders in the Rue Morgue," in which Auguste Dupin solves murders caused by a mysterious, inhuman predator. But Poe also had a wicked sense of humor and a stinging wit that often appeared in many of his short stories. This side of the poet is shown best in a hilarious and occasionally horrifying short story called "The System of Doctor Tarr and Professor Fether."

Like many fabulists, Poe was intrigued by real-life mysteries, including the conspiracy-minded theory of a Hollow Earth inhabited by superior beings. The theory was advanced by John Symmes, an army officer and explorer who believed there were vast openings at the North and South Poles.

Poe set his characters adrift on an expedition to find an opening at the pole. After a catastrophe on ship, only four survivors were left alive, drifting on the icy antarctic waters on a small boat. Included among the survivors was a cabin boy named Richard Parker, who was cannibalized by the other survivors.

This situation was mirrored almost half a century later when a real-life shipwreck left four survivors in a boat—including a cabin boy named Richard Parker who was cannibalized by his *real-life* shipmates.

In the real-life case, the survivors were tried for the murder of Richard Parker.

A detailed account of Poe's investigations into the Hollow Earth theory and the material he used as inspiration for *The Narrative of Arthur Gordon Pym* can be found in Walter Kafton-Minkel's thoroughly researched and thought-provoking book *Subterranean Worlds: 100,000 Years of Dragons, Dwarfs, the Dead, Lost Races, & UFOS From Inside the Earth*.

An equally fascinating book is Alan Vaughn's *Incredi-*

*ble Coincidences*, which provides one of the best accounts of Poe's Richard Parker character and the real-life cabin boy who suffered the same fate.

*Incredible Coincidences* also covers other unusual correlations between prophetic fiction and fact, including the novel *Black Abduction*, by Harrison James, which presaged Patty Hearst's abduction by the Symbionese Liberation Army, and Morgan Robertson's novel *The Wreck of the Titan*, which preceded the sinking of the *Titanic* by fourteen years.

# SELECTED
# BIBLIOGRAPHY

Baigent, Michael, Richard Leigh, and Henry Lincoln. *Holy Blood, Holy Grail*. Dell Publishing Co., Inc., 1983.

Birnbaum, Stephen. *Birnbaum's Europe 1988*. Houghton Mifflin Company, 1987.

Birnbaum, Stephen. *Birnbaum's South America 1990*. Houghton Mifflin Company, 1989.

Bleeker, Sonia. *The Inca: Indians of the Andes*. William Morrow & Company, 1960.

Blumenson, Martin. *Patton: The Man Behind the Legend, 1885–1945*. William Morrow, 1985.

Blundell, Nigel. *The World's Greatest Mysteries*. Exeter Books, 1984.

Bulfinch, Thomas. *The Age of Chivalry and Legends of Charlemagne*. The New American Library of World Literature, Inc., 1962.

Cantril, Hadley. *The Invasion From Mars: A Study in the Psychology of Panic*. Princeton University Press, 1940.

Cavendish, Richard. *Legends of the World*. Crescent Books, 1989.

Chidsey, Donald Barr. *Valley Forge: An On-the-Scene Account of the Winter Crisis in the Revolutionary War*. Crown, 1959.

Cohen, Daniel. *The Encyclopedia of Ghosts*. Dodd, Mead and Company, 1984.

Collins, John Stewart. *Christopher Columbus*. Stein and Day, 1977.

Connell, Evan S. *A Long Desire*. Holt Rinehart & Winston, 1979.

Daraul, Arkon. *A History of Secret Societies*. Citadel Press, 1961.

Davis Wade. *The Serpent and the Rainbow*. Simon and Schuster, 1985.

de Las Casas, Bartomelé, (trans. by Andree Collard). *History of the Indies*. Torchbook Library, 1971.

Drury, Nevill. *Dictionary of Mysticism and the Occult*. Harper & Row, Publishers, Inc., 1985.

Fairbairn, Neil. *Kingdoms of Arthur*. Spectator Publications, 1983.

Flornoy, Bertrand. *The World of the Inca*. The Vanguard Press, 1956.

Foner, Laura, and Eugene Genovese. *Slavery in the New World*. Prentice-Hall, Inc., 1969.

Gallery Books. *The World's Most Infamous Crimes and Criminals*. W. H. Smith Publishers, Inc., 1987.

Gifford, Stanley M. *Fort William Henry, A History*. 1955, A historical booklet available at the fort, Lake George, New York.

Goldston, Robert. *Satan's Disciples*. Ballantine Books, Inc., 1962.

Grolier Incorporated. *The New Book of Knowledge*. 1989.

Guirdham, Arthur. *The Cathars and Reincarnation*. Neville Spearman, 1970.

Guirdham, Arthur. *We Are One Another*. Neville Spearman, 1974.

Hook, Donald. *Madmen of History*. Dorset Press, 1986.

Howard, Michael. *The Occult Conspiracy*. Destiny Books, 1989.

Hoyt, Edwin P. *America's Wars and Military Excursions*. McGraw-Hill Book Company, 1987.

Hurwood, Bernhardt J. *Strange Lives*. Popular Library, 1966.

Kafton-Minkel, Walter. *Subterranean Worlds: 100,000 Years of Dragons, Dwarfs, the Dead, Lost Races, & UFOS From Inside the Earth*. Loompanics Unlimited, 1989.

Kohn, George C. *Dictionary of Wars*. Facts on File Publications, 1986.

Lacy, Norris J. *The Arthurian Encyclopedia*. Garland Publishing, 1986.

Lindstrom, Bjorn. *Columbus: The Story of Don Cristobal Colon*. Macmillan, 1966.

Louda, Jiri, and Michael Maclagan. *Heraldry of the Royal Families of Europe*. Orbis Publishing/Clarkson N. Potter, Inc., 1981.

McCall, Andrew. *The Medieval Underworld*. Hamish Hamilton, 1979.

Mackay, Charles. *Extraordinary Popular Delusions and the Madness of Crowds*. Harmony Books, 1980.

Matthews, John, and Bob Stewart. *Warriors of Christendom*. Firebird Books, 1988.

Metraux, Alfred. *The History of the Incas*. Random House, 1969.

Mills, Dorothy. *The Middle Ages*. G. P. Putnam's Sons, 1935.

Mitchell, John. *The New View Over Atlantis*. Harper & Row, 1983.

Moncrieff, A.R. Hope. *Romance and Legend of Chivalry*. Crescent Books, 1986.

Monmouth, Geoffrey, (trans. by Lewis Thorpe). *The History of the Kings of Britain*. Penguin Books, 1963.

Myles, Douglas. *Prince Dracula: Son of the Devil*. McGraw-Hill Book Company, 1988.

Nash, Jay Robert. *Look for the Woman*. M. Evans and Company, Inc., 1981.

*The New York Times*. Various editions 1881–1882 and 1915–1921.

Newark, Tim. *Medieval Warlords*. Blandford Press, 1987.

Nigg, Walter. *The Heretics*. Dorset Press, 1990.

Oldenbourg, Zoe. *Massacre at Montsegur: A History of the Albigensian Crusade*. Dorset Press, 1990.

Owen, Gale R. *Rites and Religions of the Anglo-Saxons*. Dorset Press, 1985.

Parkman, Francis. *Wolfe and Montcalm*. Little Brown and Co., 1884.

Parrinder, Geoffrey (edited). *World Religions: From An-*

*cient History to the Present*. Facts on File Publications, 1971.

Patton, General George S. *War As I Knew It*. Houghton, Mifflin and Company, 1947.

Platnick, Kenneth. *Great Mysteries of History*. Dorset Press, 1972.

Prescott, William H. *History of the Conquest of Mexico and History of the Conquest of Peru*. The Modern Library, a division of Random House, Inc. (undated edition).

Price, Mary R., and Margaret Howell. *From Barbarism to Chivalry*. Oxford University Press, 1972.

Radcliff, Virgina. *The Caribbean Heritage*. Walker and Co., 1976.

Rainey, Richard. *Phantom Forces*. Berkley Books, 1990.

Ravenscroft, Trevor. *The Spear of Destiny*. Bantam Books, Inc., 1973.

Richards, Duncan, and Patrice Milleron (edited). *The Hachette Guide to France*. Pantheon Books, 1985.

Robbins, Rossell Hope. *The Encyclopedia of Witchcraft and Demonology*. Bonanza Books, 1981.

Rubinsky, Yuri, and Ian Wiseman. *History of the End of the World*. Quill Books, 1982.

Skinner, Charles. *Myths and Legends of Our Own Land*. J.B. Lippincott Company, 1896.

Stern, Jess. *The Door to the Future*. Doubleday and Co., 1963.

Stewart, Louis. *Life Forces: A Contemporary Guide to the Cult and Occult*. Andrews and McMeel, Inc., 1980.

Stevenson, Kenneth E., and Gary R. Habermas. *Verdict on the Shroud*. Banbury Books, 1984.

Stevenson, Robert Louis. *Ticonderoga: A Legend of the West Highlands*. Booklet printed for The Fort Ticonderoga Museum, 1947. With permission of Charles Scribner's Sons, 1887.

Tappan, Eva March. *When Knights Were Bold*. Houghton Mifflin Company, 1911.

Time-Life Books. *Psychic Voyages, Mysteries of the Unknown*. Time-Life Books, Inc., 1987.

Time-Life Books. *Visions and Prophecies, Mysteries of the Unknown*. Time-Life Books, Inc., 1988.

Thorndike, Lynn, Ph.D. *The History of Medieval Europe*. Houghton Mifflin Company, 1917.

Thorpe, Lewis (trans). *Einhard and Notker the Stammerer: Two Lives of Charlemagne*. Penguin, 1969.

Van de Water, Frederic F. *Lake Champlain and Lake George*. Bobbs-Merrill Company, 1946.

Vaughan, Alan. *Incredible Coincidence: The Baffling World of Synchronicity*. Ballantine Books, 1979.

von Hagen, Victor W. *The Incas: People of the Sun*. The World Publishing Company, 1961.

Wallechinsky, David, and Irving Wallace. *The People's Almanac*. Doubleday & Company, 1975.

Wallechinsky, David, and Irving Wallace. *The People's Almanac #2*. Bantam Books, Inc., 1978.

Walvin, James. *Slavery and the Slave Trade*. University Press, 1983.

Wells, H.G. *The Outline of History: The Whole Story of Man*. Doubleday & Company, Inc., 1971.

Wilgus, Neal. *The Illuminoids*. Pocket Books, 1978.

Wilson, Colin, and Damon Wilson. *The Encyclopedia of Unsolved Mysteries*. Contemporary Books, Inc., 1988.

Wilson, Ian. *Undiscovered*. Beech Tree Books, 1983.

Wright, John W. *The Universal Almanac*. Andrews and McMeel, 1989.

Wrong, George M. *Washington and His Comrades in Arms: A Chronicle of the War of Independence*. Yale University Press, 1921.

Zach, Paul. *Jamaica*. APA Publications, 1989.